Outrage
Strike Force X: Book Two

MICHAEL NEWTON

WOLFPACK PUBLISHING
— EST 2013 —

WOLFPACK
PUBLISHING
— EST 2013 —

Published in the United States by Wolfpack Publishing, Las Vegas

Wolfpack Publishing
6032 Wheat Penny Avenue
Las Vegas, NV 89122

wolfpackpublishing.com

Paperback ISBN 978-1-64734-053-7
Kindle ISBN 978-1-64734-052-0

Library of Congress Number: 2020943386

Outrage

For Angelo and Esme

"They've done it before and they'll do it again and when they do it, seems that only the children weep."

Harper Lee, *To Kill a Mockingbird*

"It only takes one mistake, and nothing else you ever do will matter. No matter how hard you work or how smart you become, you'll always be known for that one poor choice. Do that one wrong thing- and you'll be dead for the rest of your life."

Chuck Palahniuk, *Snuff*

1

SoHo, Manhattan

SoHo was slamming, and The Red Zone club on Spring Street, between Hudson and Varick, was no exception, packed wall-to-wall with revelers determined to party hearty until closing time at 4:00 a.m.

SoHo—shorthand for "South of Houston Street" since 1962—has variable boundaries, depending on the source consulted, and has passed through phases like Manhattan's other neighborhoods. Originally farmland ceded to freed slaves before there was a USA, it harbored industry and thriving brothels in the Civil War that ultimately freed all slaves, was dubbed "Hell's Hundred Acres" in the 1950s, saw its many cast iron buildings tagged as historical treasures a decade later, then was "gentrified" with artists' lofts and nightclubs meant to swing as if there might be no tomorrow.

One of those, The Red Zone, seemed to take that ethos seriously.

On this manic Saturday, a hometown "doom metal" band called Dying Light was hammering eardrums and rattling liquor bottles at a decibel level unsafe for human eardrums. Conversation wasn't totally impossible during the group's explosive sets, but it required shouting from point-blank range and would have benefitted greatly from subtitles.

Not that anybody came to The Red Zone for simple chit-chat. Never had and never would.

The club, without apologies, was a committed hookup joint. Patrons might find an unintended soul mate, although most came looking for a one-night stand or wild weekend. They also came in search of dealers pushing everything from weed and ecstasy (the MDMA kind) to coke and heroin, with a sideline in Rohypnol to aid the socially impaired with bagging semiconscious "dates." Narcs made a move inside the Zone from time to time, but they could never prove that management condoned or even knew a thing about sale of illicit chemicals onsite.

You took your chances at The Red Zone and most patrons recognized that going in. The more naïve seemed satisfied to roll the dice and risk their futures for a night of fun and frolic on the town.

Take Carrie and Michelle, two coeds from Columbia U in Morningside Heights, sandwiched between Harlem and the Upper West Side. They were typical Red Zone habitués, making the scene a couple nights per week on average, spending the money that their well-off parents had earmarked for books, tuition, campus housing and the like. Brunette Carrie and blonde Michelle made perfect bookends, every randy fellow's vision of a threesome in the making, but they'd skated on thin ice without a serious mishap so far and carried condoms on SoHo safaris, just to keep things reasonably safe.

Until tonight.

Both twenty-one-year-olds were two sheets to the wind, at least, and trying hard to hoist a third, enjoying fruity drinks and Dying Light's dubious talents, giggling at nothing much in general and shouting back and forth when random thoughts required communication. They had fallen in with two slick dudes, who'd introduced themselves as Rick and Devon, saving pocket money when the guys agreed to spring for drinks, presumably in hopes of getting laid.

It might or might now go that way, depending on what Carrie and Michelle decided later, but at half-past midnight they were simply having fun.

Or Michelle was, at least. Her campus roomie, not so much.

Now, suddenly and unexpectedly, Carrie was feeling groggy, going on dizzy, well beyond her normal state after downing three or four cocktails. In fact, her roiling stomach made her wonder if the sushi she'd divided with Michelle before they hit The Red Zone might have been a trifle past its sell-by date.

Last thing she needed now was food poisoning, piled on top of all the other problems she was drinking to forget—or, at the very least, to put on hold for one more night.

Ignoring Rick and Devon, Carrie leaned in kissing close and told Michelle, hating the warble in her voice, "Feel sick. I'm heading for the loo."

She'd picked up British slang for restrooms somewhere in the past couple of years but hadn't got around to calling elevators "lifts" so far. "Loo" was about as continental as she cared to be just now.

Carrie knew where the Red Zone's restrooms were located, past the stage and shoved into the nightclub's northeast corner, sporting door signs reading "HIS" and "HERS." She wobbled toward them now, apologizing in a muted voice to dancers she collided with along the way, and feared her skull might detonate from the concussive blast of Dying Light's big Boss Katana amplifiers.

That turned out to be a false alarm, although a painful one. She made it to the door marked "HERS," pushed through, and zombie-walked to a Naugahyde-covered divan near a bank of six sinks. On other visits to the ladies' room she'd seen the sofa hosting girl-on-girl action a time or two, but this time Carrie had it to herself. She sat, leaned back against the wall's cool tile, and waited for the room to cease its spinning.

Waited, and then waited some more. Instead of easing up though, whatever was happening to Carrie wasn't letting up. If anything, she felt it getting worse, as if about to carry her away.

The door swung open, and next thing she knew, a sympathetic-looking girl around her own age was beside her, warm hand on her bare shoulder, asking, "You okay, Hon? Hate to say it, but you aren't looking too good."

Back in The Zone's main room Michelle was now concerned enough about Carrie to sober up a bit and set her cocktail down unfinished on the bar. Waiting for a break in Dying Light's song "Contin Seed"—number ninety-seven with an anchor on the Hot 100 chart—she bent toward Rick or Devon, virtually interchangeable, and asked him, "Have you seen Carrie?"

He blinked and seemed about to ask her, "Who?" then caught himself in time and answered, "Nope. You want me go and find her for ya?"

"Maybe I should," she replied. "You can't go in the ladies' for a look around."

"No sweat, Babe. I'll snag someone going in and have 'em check."

"Okay, then. Thanks!"

The band lashed out again with "Hell and Gone," while Rick or Devon slipped away into the crowd. Michelle picked up her drink and told Devon or Rick where his wing man had gone.

"Cool, Babe. He's like some kinda tracking dog, you know?"

She thought he had the dog part right but settled for a smile and nod.

It was a royal pain, Carrie coming down with something if that proved to be the case. Not only would Michelle have to consider catching it herself, but it meant dragging Carrie out to catch a taxi if she found one waiting, maybe call an Uber if there wasn't one. A nine-mile drive would cost her fifteen dollars in a cab, not counting any tip she could afford, or roughly double that for Uber with the booking charge and all. She planned to put it on her daddy's credit card, but still…

And what if Carrie tossed her cookie in the car? Toss in a cleanup fee Michelle couldn't begin to guesstimate.

The band was kicking into "666," howling about the Number of the Beast, when she turned back to Rick or Devon, telling him, "I'd better go and look for her myself."

"Okay, Babe. Want some company?"

"Whatever."

She moved off to find the restrooms, navigating around couples, trios and quartets dancing or taking up floor space to run their gums. Assessing how she felt, Michelle checked off the box for tipsy but felt nothing to indicate she'd caught a bug from Carrie. If the sushi had been off, she figured that it should be hitting her by now, so that was something to be thankful for, at least.

A glance back showed her Rick or Devon weaving through The Red Zone's thronging customers, a few yards short of keeping up with her. Not caring, she pushed on, hoping to find her roommate coming out of whatever had nudged her equilibrium off-kilter. Otherwise, Michelle would have to manage getting Carrie from the club out to the curb, finesse a ride, then drag her back into the dorm and put her into bed, hopefully dodging any mess along the way.

She hesitated for a moment at the entrance to the ladies' room, then looked around once more and saw that Rick or Devon had caught up with her. He was distracted, watching as a goth girl in a straining black tank top passed by, and with an eye-roll, Michelle blew him off. She entered, found nobody on the sofa to her right, and started checking toilet stalls.

Eight doors, all shut, but no feet showing under any of them as she moved along the line. Reaching the end, she called out, "Carrie? Are you in here?" Feeling stupid, since she plainly isn't, unless something has persuaded her to lift her feet and hide.

Another pass along the stalls, this time pushing each door in turn and seeing toilets without occupants.

"Now what?" she asked herself but got no answer in return.

She left the ladies, almost hit a couple of incoming patrons with the swinging door but didn't bother to apologize when one of them called after her, "Excuse you, bitch!"

No time to waste. She spotted Rick or Devon, poked him in the ribs, and said, "She's gone."

"Gone where?"

Dumbass, she thought. But answered back, "How would I know?"

"You're mad at *me*, now? That's not cool, Babe."

"Call me 'Babe' once more and find out how uncool I am." He took a short step backward, as she asked him, "Where's your friend?"

"Hey, Ba—" He caught himself in time. "I was with you, remember?"

"Right. Which one are you again?"

"That's cold," he said, as Dying Light slouched off the stage to take a welcome break. "I'm Rick, okay?"

"You have I.D.?"

"What, you're the heat, now?"

"Listen up. Somebody fed my friend a roofie, something, I don't know. She's gone and so's your buddy. Let me see I.D. right now, or you can damn well show it to the heat when I'm done screaming, 'Rape'!"

"Okay, Jesus! Hang on a sec, will you?"

He fished his wallet out of a back pocket, showed Michelle a New York driver's license that identified him as Rick Johnson with a home address on Staten Island. Always good at memorizing trivia, she filed that in her mind and said, "Now, do you want to help me find Carrie or tell the cops about your good friend Devon?"

Standing with shoulders slumped, defeated, he replied, "Okay. Where do we start?"

A beat-up Chevy Express Cargo van, once black, now primer-spotted, stood behind The Red Zone near a reeking dumpster in a littered alleyway. Its double doors stood open on the right hand side, a driver at the wheel, while "Devon"—not the name his parents gave him at the hospital where he was born—half-dragged unconscious Carrie toward the vehicle.

He knew the stats for ketamine administered by mouth, as in a drink. It kicked in full-bore anywhere from fifteen minutes up to thirty after being swallowed, based upon a subject's body mass, and started wearing off somewhere between one and six hours afterward. Ninety-one percent excreted through the urinary system, one to three percent in feces, while the rest metabolized.

The drug had many uses recognized by medical practitioners as being on the up-and-up: anesthetizing animals or children during surgery; relaxing muscles prior to intubation of the trachea; treating asthmatics or victims of chronic obstructive airway disease; preventing opioid-induced hyperalgesia; easing the pain of emergency surgery in wartime field conditions—the list went on and on.

Additionally, and what had suited pseudo-Devon's needs tonight at The Red Zone, it was a first-rate Mickey Finn for date rapes and abductions. A few drops in some honey's cocktail, and within a short half hour she was down the K-hole, helpless as a sacrificial lamb.

Just what the doctor—or the buyer—ordered in this case.

"You sure this is the right one?" asked a hulking shadow

from the van's interior, before he took the handoff from his sidekick in the alley.

"Damn sure," said the victim's escort, known to her but briefly by a name that wasn't his. "I've got her purse here. Check the driver's license."

From the sidelines, just emerging from behind the nearby garbage bin, a third participant declared, "It's her, all right. Get on with it before the drug starts wearing off."

A woman's voice.

"We're cool, ma'am," the ex-Devon told her. "Earned our payoff five-by-five."

"You'll get your payoff when the deal's done, as agreed," the shadow-women said. "And not a minute sooner."

"What I meant, sure. Absolutely."

"So get on with it. Stop wasting time."

Inside the Chevrolet, the hulk gripped Carrie by one arm and hauled her up into the van, dropping her flaccid body on a cheap air mattress, bending down to cuff her wrists and pull a burlap sack over her head.

"Be careful you don't suffocate her," said the female bystander. "At least, not yet."

The driver might have laughed at that, or maybe he was just clearing his throat. In either case, the watching woman didn't care.

"You coming with?" asked pseudo-Devon. "Plenty room in here, yo."

"Let me guess," she sneered at him. "You weren't an English major?"

"No major at all, ma'am," fake Devon replied. "I didn't make the grades and couldn't swing tuition anyhow."

"Check out a correspondence course when this is over," she advised. "Make something of yourself."

"Huh?"

"Forget it. Use the route we planned. I'll follow you, and you can count on being watched in transit."

"Sure, ma'am. We've been over all of that six ways from Sunday."

"For your sake, I hope so," said the woman. "Deviate in any way and you'll be written out for good. No payday, no tomorrows. Squat."

Faux Devon bobbed his head and climbed into the van, pausing to close its sliding door before the driver revved his 5.7-liter Vortec V8 engine and rolled out of there. The woman paused to light up a Virginia Slim, then walked back to her car, parked well clear of the alley's only pole lamp, trailing smoke behind her.

So far, it was going down all right, not hitches, but she couldn't sit back and relax until the deed was done. At that point, it would be time to dispense with some dead wood.

And she knew just exactly who should wield the axe.

In fact, she thought, that might be fun to watch.

Michelle was seriously worried now.

Carrie was flighty, sure, and often irresponsible, but there was no way she'd just up and disappear without a word, leaving Michelle in The Red Zone, particularly when she'd looked and acted like an extra from *The Walking Dead* when she went off to use the ladies' room.

No way at all.

Aside from being roommates and best friends, Michelle and Carrie had an iron-clad pact that neither one of them would ever ditch the other at a gin joint without talking through a firm advance plan. One-night things were cool— even a doubleheader in their dorm room on the odd occasion, but just taking off without a word would never enter Carrie's mind, no matter how drunk she might be.

Unless she wasn't simply drunk but stoned on something that she hadn't meant to take.

Unless it hadn't been her plan to leave the club at all.

Michelle tried Carrie's cell first thing, after her strikeout in the ladies', but it went to voicemail with the same recorded message she had heard a thousand times before, at least. Carrie never went anywhere without her phone—bathrooms included—and Michelle had seen her carrying the clutch purse that contained it when she'd lurched off to the "loo."

There's been no purse lying around the ladies' when she'd checked it out, either. Wherever Carrie had gone off to, voluntarily or otherwise, her phone had also made the trip.

Another try, another call diverted to voicemail. That time, Michelle had hissed over the line, "You'd better call me back right now, damn it!"

But no return call came.

Another fifteen minutes waiting, scouring The Red Zone for a glimpse of Carrie with half-hearted aid from Rick, proved fruitless. Flashing strobes and blaring music made the club a little slice of Hell on Earth, as the proprietor doubtless intended, but the leaping shadows weren't concealing Carrie at a corner table, in a booth, or at the bar where drinkers stood three-deep. She'd simply vanished, blinked out of existence somehow in the fifty feet between the last place that Michelle had spoken to her and the ladies' room.

Enough stalling.

Michelle keyed up her cell again but didn't try Carrie this time. Instead, she tapped three numbers: 911.

Rick didn't know what she was doing. Said, "She would've answered you by now, I'm thinking."

"If she could," Michelle replied. "That's why I'm calling the police."

"Hey, now!" he protested. "Don't get carried away, yo. We can wait a little while and—"

"Screw that, *yo*," she interrupted him. "I'm calling and you're staying here to meet them."

"Yeah, Or what?"

"Or they'll be knocking on your door before the night's out," she replied. "Got anything at home that might embarrass you when they show up? Like maybe land your ass at Rikers Island?"

"Totally uncool."

"Shut up and wait."

She had an operator on the line, inquiring as to her emergency. Michelle laid out the story, short and sweet, then had to answer three quick questions.

Where was she? Had she been drinking? Were Michelle and Carrie both of legal age to hang in bars?

Yes, yea, and yes.

"Ma'am, is there any chance she left without you seeing her?" the NYPD operator asked.

"No way!" Michelle replied, anger warming her cheeks. "She told me she was feeling sick and headed for the restroom, and she's missing now. You get it? I think someone spiked her drink. We need a team down here right now!"

"Unfortunately, ma'am, a person twenty-one or older is at liberty to give her friends the slip."

"She wouldn't—"

"And state law requires police to wait twenty-four hours on an adult missing-person case, unless we have a witness to foul play."

"Great! I'm your witness. I just told you—"

"That your friend was feeling queasy after drinking. If you didn't see her physically abducted from the bar, then I'm afraid you didn't witness anything that waives the legal deadline for investigation."

Deadline. Michelle didn't like the sound of that at all.

"But I—"

"Ma'am, did you check around outside the bar, to see if your friend went to get some air after she visited the restroom?"

"No, but—"

"That would be my next suggestion for you. After that,

unless you've found some evidence a criminal offense has been committed, I'm afraid our hands are tied under the law."

"Listen, will you? Carrie's not just some drunk you can write off!"

"Ma'am, we're not writing anybody off, I promise you. I'm filing your report and a recording of this call will be maintained. Aside from special circumstances—an abducted minor, senior citizen at risk, etcetera—active investigation will be handled by the First Precinct as mandated by New York statutes."

"You don't understand!"

"Ma'am, if there's no more you can add tonight—"

"My friend's parents are bigshots, get it? You have no freaking idea!"

"Ma'am—"

"Save it! I'm calling them myself. This time tomorrow, you might be a meter-maid in Bed-Stuy."

She cut the link, fuming. Beside her, Rick was watching with a glum expression on his mug.

"Sounds like that didn't go so well," he said.

"Stay where you are," Michelle ordered. "Don't even *think* you're bailing out on this!"

"On *what*, yo? We don't know that anything has happened. If it *has*, I've got nothing to do with it."

"You try to leave, I give the heat your name, address and driver's license number. Nod if you can understand me."

Rick's head bobbed and he didn't try to move away.

"Who are you calling now?" he asked her, as Michelle began to speed-dial yet another number saved onto her cell.

"Carrie's father," she said. "If he can't shake things up, nobody can."

2

The Daniel Patrick Moynihan United States Courthouse stands at 500 Pearl Street in the Civic Center neighborhood of Lower Manhattan. It is the second largest U.S. courthouse in America, after the Thomas F. Eagleton federal court in St. Louis, looming twenty-seven stories tall, housing 974,000 interior square feet, including forty-four courtrooms with their supporting office space and holding cells for prisoners awaiting trial.

Opened in 1996, the courthouse is one of four serving the Southern District of New York, a jurisdiction that encompasses eight counties and two of Gotham's five boroughs. Manhattan hosts two courthouses; two others operate from White Plains and Poughkeepsie, drawing jurors randomly from all eight counties as their turns arise.

Once a "leisurely one-man court," the Southern District has expended since its first session convened in November 1789, its jurists hearing cases that included damage claims arising from the sinking of the ships *Titanic* and *Lusitania,* the Cold War spying trials of Alger Hiss, Elizbeth Bentley and the later-executed Rosenbergs, plus government bids to block publication of James Joyce's novel *Ulysses* and *New*

York Times publication of the Pentagon Papers, followed by the Mafia "Commission Trial" that jailed nine leaders of New York's "Five Families" in 1986.

Manhattan is a long way from headquarters of the SFX Corporation in Southern California; twenty-eight hundred miles as the Boeing 747 flies from San Diego International to JFK in Queens. Urgent calls from the Department of Justice settled the itinerary, although details of the job remained obscure.

Someone in trouble; that was understood. Beyond that, they would have to wait and see.

On paper, SFX had no more formal name and didn't stand for anything specific. To its members it was Strike Force X, not indicating tenth in line by any means, but rather "X" as in anonymous. Out west, not far from La-La Land, it didn't hurt that "SFX" was also movie-speak for "special effects," which were in fact the corporation's stock in trade.

It was a private military company, much smaller than the giants that grabbed headlines pro and con—Blackwater (now Academi), Aegis Defense Services, Sandline International, the global list went on and on—but there were times when compact size coupled with peerless expertise was just exactly what the doctor ordered.

SFX's mastermind was Grant Mahoney, thirty-three years old, a veteran commando of the U.S. Army's 1st Special Forces Operational Detachment-Delta, popularly known as Delta Force. Upon his separation from the service he'd conceived the plan for SFX and served the company as CEO and CFO.

Grant's brother, Blake Mahoney, two years younger, was a former U.S. Navy SEAL, Vice President of SFX, and Grant's frequent competitor since they were old enough to walk, then run and scuffle over anything that came to mind. In his spare time away from SFX, Blake earned side money as a professional MMA cage fighter, under the pseudonym of "Michael Blake." His matches had been featured globally on pay-per-view TV with nobody the wiser as to his connection with the San Diego firm.

Third up and "old man" of the team at forty, Briton Reginald Hardy was a decorated veteran of his homeland's Special Air Service, a designated marksman—the modern euphemism for a sniper in polite society—and all-around guerilla warrior. When he wasn't working on a job for SFX, Hardy's first love was teaching "Third World" wildlife wardens the fine points of stalking poachers in the wild and preferably leaving them behind as food for scavengers. Aside from English, Reg was fluent in German, Swahili, Cantonese and Mandarin.

Stanley Dartnell, Australian-born, was thirty-seven and had served his tours of duty with the Special Operations Command, an elite unit within the Australian Defense Force. He kept his head shaved but wore wigs if needed for a given undercover role, along with facial hair in styles that could have fooled a Hollywood expert. He'd lost the tip of his left pinky finger in a knife fight where his adversary wound up losing everything. Aside from native English, Stan was fluent in French, Korean, Malay and Tagalog, a widespread Austronesian language heavily influenced by colonial-era Spanish.

Last and youngest member of the team at twenty-nine was Natalie Karpin, a sabra born in Israel on Yom Kippur 1991. Before retiring into private service, she'd spent time with the Israeli Defense Force's General Staff Reconnaissance Unit, sometimes called Unit 69, more often Sayeret Matkal. Expert with small arms and explosives, she also held a black belt in the "dirty fighting" methods of *krav magda*. Given the location of her birth and military service, Natalie was fluent in English, Hebrew, Arabic, Urdu and Russian.

They rode together in a limousine bearing plates that read "U.S. GOVERNMENT—FOR OFFICIAL USE ONLY." When it reached the courthouse they piled out and started up the concrete steps, Natalie asking no one in particular,

"So who's this senator, again?"

Grant answered, "Harlan Maddox, sixty-two years old and he's spent half that time in Congress, first elected to the Senate in 2001, riding the wave from 9/11. He's Virginia's senior senator today and an established D.C. power broker, chairman of the Appropriations Committee, co-chairman of Homeland Security and Governmental Affairs, and a senior member of Judiciary Committee."

"You knew all that or looked him up, mate?" asked Dartnell.

"A bit of both," Mahoney granted. "I can tell you that he lost his first wife five years back, to cancer, and remarried soon thereafter to the current Mrs. Maddox, twenty-six years younger. There's a daughter from the first marriage, no other kids. Jolene, wife number two, was what some used to call a 'B' actress in movies and TV, back in the late Nineties, then did a bit of modeling but never hit it big."

"The senator requested us, specifically?" Reg Hardy asked.

"Don't ask me why," Grant said. "The DOJ is keeping this one on the downlow till we sit down with them face-to-face."

"And who all's coming?" brother Blake inquired.

Grant shrugged, trying to keep it casual. "I guess you'll find out with the rest of us."

A U.S. marshal wearing court credentials clipped to his lapel was waiting for them in the lobby, greeting them without the offer of a handshake, steering them past a seven-pillared tribute to "New York's Moynihan" on loan from the Museum of New York City to a bank of elevators on their left. He pushed a button, ushered them aboard the next car to arrive, and saw them off while talking through his cuff to someone high above, saying, "They're coming up right now."

Another marshal, this one female, met them on their designated floor and walked them to a conference room, rapped on the door, and held it open for them when a gruff voice ordered, "Come!"

Six men and one woman occupied one end of a table ringed by twenty chairs. Without awaiting invitations, members of the SFX team sat around the far end, facing the mismatched committee members from a range of thirty feet or so.

"I guess we weren't expecting quite so many," one of the presumed feds offered.

"We're the team you called for," Grant Mahoney answered. "There's nobody else."

"Well, then," the same first speaker said, "if you could make the introductions?"

"You first," Grant replied, "since we've already flown the best part of three thousand miles at your request."

The man who'd greeted them, after a fashion, blinked at that, then forced a smile and said, "Why not? I'm Harold Duchene, FBI Assistant Director in Charge for New York City. We already spoke, if you're Mr. Mahoney."

"One of them," Grant said..

He knew that Gotham's field office had grown so much from its humble beginning in 1908 that it rated an assistant director, rather than one of the SACs—special agents in charge—who ran the country's other bureau offices aside from those in Los Angeles and D.C., which some old-timers still referred to as the "Seat of Government." Duchene was in his early fifties, hair graying around the temples, but seemed fit enough to grapple with a public enemy unaided by subordinates.

"Immediately to my left," Duchene went on, "this is Dwayne Ralston, Assistant U.S. Attorney General for the DOJ's Office of Legislative Affairs, up from Washington."

Ralston appeared to be at least a dozen years Duchene's junior, but soft and balding. At his present rank, he'd spend most days behind a desk, finessing issues between Justice and Congress. A pair of wire-rimmed glassed magnified his rheumy eyes.

"To Mr. Ralston's left," Duchene continued, "is Adele Wainwright, Deputy Attorney General for the Southern District of New York."

The lady was a year or two older than Ralston and had kept herself in better shape, discreetly made-up, ash blond hair recently styled and sparing no expense. She wore no jewelry that Grant could see except for pinprick diamond earrings. Her Givenchy business suit was cut conservatively but still snug enough to show she had it going on.

"At the head of the table," Duchene continued, "we have—"

"Senator Maddox requires no introduction," Grant cut in, "although we've never met before. We all have TV sets at home."

Maddox's face remained deadpan beneath immaculately styled white hair, but something clearly was disturbing him, gnawing away behind his eyes.

"Right, then," the FBI man said. "Across the table from Ms. Wainwright, meet Liam Byrne, Chief of Detectives for NYPD, in from One Police Plaza.

Mahoney had prepared for the occasion with a dress uniform bearing three gold stars on its epaulets. While expensively cut, the dress blues smelled of cigars and couldn't hide the fact that he was twenty-five pounds overweight, at least. Above bushy black eyebrows, the detective's hairline was retreating toward his crown.

"And finally," Duchene announced, "Carmine Alesio, NHPD's Chief of Intelligence."

The second cop on hand was also wearing a three-starred dress uniform, but he was whip-thin, swarthy, his full head of dark hair oiled and combed back from his slender face. An old, pale scar ran from the outside corner of his left eye toward his ear.

"Okay, then," said Mahoney, wasting no time on reciting military records as he introduced the other members of his team, saving himself for last. Already tired of waiting, he addressed himself to the assembled feds and local lawmen, saying, "Someone want to tell us what we're doing here?"

Duchene turned toward the table's head. "Senator?"

"Right," Maddox. "My daughter's been abducted under threat of death, and so far no one in this room, with all the troops at their disposal, spending millions every hour, has done anything about it."

That set off a grumbling furor at the far end of the table, everyone except Adele Wainwright protesting that they'd done their level best so far and couldn't be responsible if those behind the kidnapping had done a first-rate job of covering their tracks. Wainwright, of course, had no responsibility until the perpetrators were identified and charged, at which point she would either oversee their prosecution personally or, more likely, delegate it to one of her slick subordinates while lurking on the sidelines.

Grant was disinclined to interrupt the verbal melee—not his place, for one thing, since he held no rank outside of SFX—and he found it instructive watching as the scene played out, allowing him to judge which members of their welcoming committee carried the most weight.

NYPD's two spokesmen clearly weren't in charge, although both clamored that their separate departments had done everything humanly possible to trace the missing girl, still unidentified by name, and run down her abductors. G-man Duchene wasn't about to contradict the cops, but he still stressed his bureau's primacy in terms of technical surveillance methods, forensic analysis and psychological profiling.

That last bit scored him no points, considering how badly shrinks had muffed profiles of serial offenders ranging from the "Boston Strangler" in the 1960s, through the L.A. "Skid Row Slasher" ten years later and that city's "Skid Row Stabber" and the "Zodiac" (both still at large, if not deceased by now), on to Atlanta's "Child Killer," convicted only in the deaths of two adult males, while some twenty-odd cases with minor victims never went to trial.

The wrangling went on until Senator Maddox struck the table with an open palm and brought it screeching to a halt. "This is my story," he informed the five unhappy people flanking him. "I'll tell it my way."

"Absolutely, Senator," Duchene chimed in. "Over to you."

Maddox addressed himself to Grant primarily but let his steely eyes rove back and forth over the other SFX team members as he launched into the spiel he'd doubtless offered up at least a dozen times before.

"Carrie's my only child," he said. "She's twenty-three years old, a student at Columbia. I won't deny she's waffled on her choice of majors, had a few false starts, and hasn't graduated yet. The school could care less, with me picking up the tab, but her grades have been slipping for a while. Sewing too many wild oats, which I guess she gets from her old man. Since this term started, she's been on academic probation, trying to fly right—or so I thought."

A moment's hesitation, then he plowed ahead. "On Saturday, she and her roommate made the rounds of certain clubs in SoHo. Around midnight they wound up at one called…what is it?" he asked the policemen seated to his right.

"The Red Zone," Chief Byrne answered on behalf of his department. "So-called heavy metal crap. Some busts for fake I.D.s and dealing on the premises but nothing we could pin on management to shut it down."

"In any case," Maddox cut in, "at some point Carrie told her friend—Michelle Boucher, by name—that she was feeling ill and went off to the women's room alone. That was the last time anyone admits to seeing her. Her roomie checked the head, found no one there, no trace of Carrie or her purse. She called my daughter's cell repeatedly. It kept going to voicemail. When she tried NYPD—" he shot a baleful glance toward the two chiefs beside him—"the response was less than helpful."

"We've looked into that," said Chief Alesio, defensively. "The nine-eleven operator was a rookie, and she gave Ms. Boucher some mistaken information. She's been disciplined."

"Should have been shit-canned," Maddox growled.

"In any case—" the second chief tried to resume.

"In *any* case," the senator talked over him, "no one could turn up anything until we got a rude surprise on Monday morning."

Duchene piped up again. "And this is where the bureau got involved," he said. "Senator, if I may...?"

"Get on with it," growled Maddox.

"Certainly." Duchene ignored the insult. Forged ahead. "We had no solid evidence of kidnapping until Senator Maddox got the ransom demand, accompanied by a short video. You'll be seeing it shortly. At that point, we took over the investigation and—"

"We're still no closer to solution of it," Maddox fumed. "I swear, I don't know what the taxpayers are getting for their money. I'm considering a round of public hearings on confused and negligent procedures. If these bastards harm a hair on Carrie's head, you'll all be wishing that you'd never heard of me."

Grant thought the various assembled law enforcement personnel were wishing that already, but he kept it to himself. Instead, he interjected, "What was the demand, sir?"

"Two-point-five million in cash," Maddox replied. "God only knows how they arrived at that figure. I'm half a million short on liquid assets, even if I sell off everything I own, but I can raise it. *Will* raise it, of course, no question. But the deadline..."

"Would be what?" Grant asked.

"Forty-eight hours, counting down from yesterday. Beyond that..."

"What?" Grant urged him on.

"See for yourself."

Maddox waved toward a giant flatscreen television on the wall to his right, or Mahoney's left. Beneath it sat a metal cart on wheels, topped with a DVD player and trailing wires up to the TV set.

"Somebody want to roll this shit?" the senator inquired and leaned back wearily into his high-backed chair.

The video was short, but no one could have called it sweet.

It started with a closeup of a man in black—ski mask and long-sleeved turtleneck—shown only from the chest up. He wore sunglasses to conceal the color of his eyes, and where his lips showed through a gap below his nose, they too were blackened, maybe by shoe polish, possible combat cosmetics used to keep an analyst from guessing race from pigmentation. On the DVD's soundtrack, distortion covered any accent, speech impediment, or other oddities that might have given him away.

His speech was short, concise.

"Hey, asshole," he began. "We have your little pretty and we know the pigs are watching this. Feel free to waste your time, Daddy. You want the little bitch back, we expect two and a half million, used bills and none of them consecutive or marked. We'll hit you back with the delivery instructions. Phone, email, we've got it all covered. If you're wondering what happens if you fuck it up, stand by to watch a sample of our work."

The screen blinked, then the video came back, this time displaying what appeared to be a cheap hotel room, possibly a basement dressed up with minimal furniture to set the scene. A naked girl, teenaged, was bound spread-eagle to single bed, ankles and wrists secured with nylon ropes. She struggled, sobbing, but seemed close to giving up.

A man came into frame, hooded and dressed in a raincoat, with blue surgical gloves. His hair and features, any scars or tattoos that he may have had, were thoroughly concealed. Even his weight was up for grabs beneath the floppy coat, where artificial padding might have been supplied to flesh him out.

He carried an electric chainsaw, its extension cord trailing away and out of sight. Pressing a button brought the saw to snarling life. His victim on the bed began to writhe and scream.

Mahoney watched the rest, revolted by it. Heard a muffled snarl from Natalie, seated beside him to his right. Knowing her sensitivity to underage and female victims, it surprised him that she didn't rise and leave the room.

When the butcher had finished with his gruesome work, spraying himself the bed and walls with gore, the screen blinked out again, then came back to its former closeup of the ski-masked narrator.

"You get the picture, Daddy? Sure you do. Pay up and get your baby back, or stall and wait to see her in the movies. We'll be cashing in, regardless. Tick-tock, asshole."

That was it, at last. Grant swallowed before saying, "So, a snuff film."

"Um, before we wander too far down that alley," said Duchene, "I feel obliged to say the bureau has investigated many claims of so-called 'snuff' films and—"

"You still keep calling them an urban legend," Maddox interrupted, almost sneering. "I keep hearing that from over-educated 'special agents' and 'consultants.' What in *hell* do you suppose we all just sat through here? Are you about to claim that poor girl didn't get the real-life *Texas Chainsaw* treatment?"

"No, sir. But we've never found—"

"Any *commercial* films," the senator broke in again. "Yeah, yeah. That will be some great consolation when these fuckers start to send my Carrie back in pieces!"

Grant had studied up on both sides of the snuff film controversy over time. The several films released to theaters and advertised as "real" had all been proven hoaxes. On the other hand, some lunatics like murder partners Leonard Lake and Charles Ng videotaped their torture slayings of abducted men and women, but the FBI stood fast, insisting that the freaks had done it for their personal amusement, not as a commercial enterprise. In 1991, erratic actor Charlie Sheen had phoned police, announcing that he'd purchased a "genuine" Japanese snuff tape that proved to be a bootleg copy of a theatrical fake.

But on the other hand, Grant was conversant with a small body of literature holding that snuff films existed and indeed demanded lofty prices from a sick, selective clientele. Israeli cop turned journalist Yaron Svoray first broke the news of death porn circulating among German neo-Nazis in 1994, with his book *In Hitler's Shadow.* Two years later, that tale was corroborated by a disillusioned fascist leader, Ingo Hasselbach, in his memoir titled *Führer-Ex.* One year after that, Svoray published his *Gods of Death,* recounting how he'd searched the globe from L.A. and New York to Paris, Germany and Bangkok, viewing several snuff films and purchasing one in Serbia before police in Belgrade seized the evidence. Along the way, he'd allegedly glimpsed method actor Robert DeNiro at a French snuff screening, conducting research, and had pinpointed a mansion in Connecticut where Wall Street oligarchs paid fifteen hundred dollars each to watch a rape-murder on film.

Some critics panned those exposés as fantasy, while conspiracy theorists claimed the FBI itself had paid now-imprisoned lady-killer Joran van der Sloot's way to Peru, where he'd purportedly taped a Satanic ritual slaying. Between those two extremes, Ted McIlvenny, director of the Institute for the Advanced Study of Human Sexuality and caretaker of the world's largest porn collection—289,000 films and 100,000 videos—insisted that he'd personally seen three films with people actually killed on camera, though two of those victims died accidentally during production of bondage or S&M scenes.

On the skeptical side, *Screw* magazine publisher Alvin

Goldstein had offered a cool million bucks for irrefutable proof of an actual snuff film, but no one applied for the bounty. So color Grant Mahoney undecided, other than the knot twisting his stomach from what he'd just witnessed onscreen.

Before the argument could run on any longer he cut in, saying, "Excuse me, people, but I have to ask exactly what you want from us right now."

Four agitated faces swung around his way, while Harlan Maddox was already facing Grant. "Nobody told you?" he demanded.

"Not so far."

Duchene began to say, "We thought it best if—"

"Screw that!" Maddox interposed. "First thing, I need someone to bring my daughter home and this bunch isn't cutting it. You think congressional committees are a mess? Try saving someone's like, someone you care about, while the so-called authorities waste precious time debating over what's real and what isn't."

Grant addressed himself to Maddox, while including all the rest. "Sir, while I understand the urgency, I mean, why us?"

"I've answered that," the senator replied. "I want my daughter back, and then I want the scum that grabbed her punished."

"Right. Except we're soldiers, not detectives. And we're certainly not prosecutors."

"I need tough professionals who aren't afraid to *act*," said Maddox. "As for prosecuting those responsible, you think they'll feel like coming in alive? They're proven murderers, most likely serial. When they resist you, take 'em out!"

"Senator, that may be how it works in Washington…"

"Don't make me laugh," the legislator scoffed. "You're mercenaries and you've served our government before. You think I, of all people, wouldn't know that?"

"In those other cases—"

"You got paid," Maddox cut in. "Do this for me, and I can guarantee the ransom that these little shits are asking for is yours."

3

East Campus Residential Complex, Columbia University

After some brief debate outside the presence of their New York hosts, most visibly reluctant now but obviously worried about irritating Harlan Maddox, members of the SFX team followed Grant Mahoney's lead and pitched in to investigate the case...at least, up to a point.

They weren't armed yet, but that was easily arranged from their established links to Gotham if the need arose. And if it *did,* all of them knew there wouldn't be a lot of time to waste. When they'd divided up the short list of potential witnesses, dispersing in three undercover vehicles NYPD supplied, Blake reached out to one of the team's contacts who worked the Brooklyn docks and put some gear on hold, available for pickup in a rush.

Natalie Karpin drew the "girl" straw, sent to meet Michelle Boucher, work through the story one more time, and see if she had inadvertently omitted anything that might be critical. After consulting a street guide, she drove eight miles due north on Route 9A from Foley Square to scout the campus at Columbia, locating the complex of dorms reserved for upper classmen at West 116th Street and Amsterdam, a short stroll from Columbia Law School. She found a parking space and put a placard on her dashboard reading NYPD OFFICER ON

DUTY, hoping that it didn't prompt some budding campus radical to vandalize her ride.

Nat had Michelle Boucher's room number, rode an elevator up to reach her floor, and followed arrows posted in the corridor to reach the double-occupancy room she'd shared with Carrie Maddox until recently. The willowy young woman who responded to her knock was five foot five, with streaked blonde hair and slouchy casual attire that wasn't managing to mask her curves.

When Karpin introduced herself and stated her business, pink color started to defuse the coed's pallid cheeks. "I talked to the police already," she said. "Same with the FBI."

"I'm playing catchup," Natalie advised. "I hope you won't mind going over it again."

"Um…no, I guess not. Come on in. The place is, well, I haven't bothered cleaning up."

"No problem."

Natalie checked out the room, a single bed against two of its four walls, open closets stuffed with clothes on hangers, shoed on racks or standing on their own. From what she saw, the friends had roughly matching fashion sense, supported by their affluent parents.

Michelle sat on her rumpled bed, while Karpin took one of the room's two straight-backed wooden chairs. They sat about three feet apart, facing each other, Boucher starting with her eyed downcast and staring at the vinyl-covered floor.

No carpet in a dorm where parties might produce long-lasting stains.

"Should I have asked to see your badge or something," Boucher asked belatedly.

"I'm an outside consultant. You can call Police Plaza and ask them to confirm it."

"Never mind." She raised her eyes to meet Karpin's. Asked her, "What do you want to know?"

"What happened as you best remember Saturday night, ending with Carrie's disappearance."

Michelle hesitated for a moment, then lifted her face, met Nat's eyes with a lone tear rolling down one cheek. "My fault," she said.

"Excuse me?"

"Going to The Red Zone. I suggested it. We'd had enough to drink already—too much, really—and we should've just come home. Back here, I mean. What if she never sees her home again?"

Natalie knew she couldn't ease that pain. Instead, she pressed, "Tell me about the guys you met there."

"Rick and Devon. I gave Rick's info to the police and FBI."

"We have that. He'll be talking to my colleagues about now."

"I checked his driver's license afterward. Too goddamned late. Devon was gone by then, along with Carrie, if that even was his name."

"What else?"

"I should've known something was wrong, the way it came on Carrie, getting sick all of a sudden. We've been out been out a lot together—too much, probably—and it's the first time anything like that has ever happened. Two of us together, there's supposed to be safety in numbers, right?"

"It doesn't always work that way, unfortunately."

"Now you tell me."

Skipping over that, Natalie said, "I've read what you told NYPD and the federals about this Devon character: dark hair, six feet or so, not heavyset, same age as Mr. Johnson, more or less. Thinking about him now, does any further information come to mind?"

"Such as?"

"Tattoos? Piercing or scars? An accent that you might identify? Something he said about himself concerning where he works or goes to school? Where he might live? A reference to other friends?"

"Sorry," Michelle replied. "My mind's a blank, besides his stupid grinning face. Smart money says he would have lied his ass off anyway. Maybe he even lied to Rick? Could that be possible?"

She sounded almost hopeful asking that, as if the thought of one more lie, one more betrayal, might finish demolishing her world.

"I couldn't say," Nat answered her. "I look forward to asking him."

"What's happening with Carrie? Has her dad heard anything?"

"We're looking into that."

"I guess her stepmom's coming on all weepy and distressed?"

"Wouldn't she be?"

"Don't buy that for a second. Carried couldn't stand her. I mean *can't*. Oh, God! Is that an omen, like? Talking about her in the past tense like she's gone for good?"

The Red Zone, SoHo

"It wouldn't be my first choice for a club's name," Blake Mahoney said.

"Trying to push the envelope, I guess," Grant answered as they stood outside the bar where Carrie Maddox had evaporated.

The "Red Zone" appellation normally applied to places where a natural disaster or intensive combat had occurred or was ongoing. During World War I the *Zone Rouge* was a part of southern France whose population had been decimated by trench warfare. Eighty-odd years later, observers hung the tag on portions of Iraq invaded by the U.S. and its allies, also the civic center of Islamabad, Pakistan, where drive-by shootings and suicide bombings were frequent. In 2011 journalists applied the label to Christchurch Central City in New Zealand, following a catastrophic earthquake that killed 185 people and sparked the declaration of a national emergency.

All bad news, all the time.

Unless it was employed to lure youngsters for a wild night on the town.

NYPD had called ahead, arranging for the club's night manager to make himself available for yet another round of questioning. From what the brothers understood, their subject—Brady Connors, two arrests for DUI, in 2010 and 2017—hadn't appreciated interruption of his beauty sleep.

Not that the brothers gave a damn.

On meeting him, Blake realized that Connors would need more than beauty sleep to make himself presentable. He dressed eccentrically for someone born and raised in Gotham, in garish floral-patterned, green cargo shorts and sandals, topped by sunglasses despite the bar's dim lighting. Unruly hair was getting close to shoulder length. All their man needed was a lei around his neck to pass for someone visiting Hawaii, maybe ducking out on mainland creditors, rather than serving as the night man at a SoHo heavy metal dive.

Connors made no attempt to shake hands during introductions. Just as well, Blake thought, seeing his nicotine-stained fingers and grimy palms that brought to mind long hours tuning cars, not stocking liquor shelves or balancing The Red Zone's books.

"Don't know what I can tell you that I haven't told the cops and feds already," he began, before the brothers asked him any questions.

Blake had already volunteered to play Bad Cop. "Why don't we start with six onsite arrests over the past two years for dealing and possession of cocaine and ecstasy?" he asked.

"Okay, let's talk about 'em," Connors said, almost defiantly. "All busts of customers, nobody on the staff. One of the six, I wasn't even hired yet. You can look it up. The rest, you gotta understand that while you may not like our customers, they still have rights."

"To peddle dope under your nose?" Blake asked.

"Hey, man." Distracted for a moment, Connors asked, "What should I call you, anyhow? Would it be 'officer' or 'agent'?"

"Stick with 'Sir'."

"Yeah, right. The thing about our Constitution's Bill of Rights is that police supposedly need warrants for a search, and businessmen like me are banned from trampling on other people's privacy, you know? Ask the Supreme Court if you don't believe me. We can't even hook out own employees up to polygraphs, to find out if they're skimming from us."

"Where'd you go to law school?" Blake inquired.

"That would be Hard Knocks University," Connors re-plied, wearing a snotty grin.

"Back to the dope arrests," Grant chimed into the conversation.

"You guys from outa town, or what?" When neither of them answered him, the night man heaved a sigh. "Look, we don't get any senior citizens unless they're cops or taxmen, right? State law requires we card patrons who reasonably might be under twenty-one. Most fake I.D.s are pretty obvious, you know? White kids paste photos on a driver's license in the name of Won Hung Lo, whatever. I've seen phony beards, mustaches, mutton chops that wouldn't fool a freshman drama student. That aside, we've got no right to pat down customers. Try that and I'd be spending all my time in court. We *do* wand hinky-looking types to make sure they're not packing guns or knives, whatever, but beyond that there's no poking, prodding, turning pockets out or looking under skirts. Our hands are tied."

"Almost like you were kidnapped," Blake observed.

"Hey, man—"

"What about date rape drugs?" Grant asked.

"I'd heard the stories, same as everybody. Ten, twelve months ago, one of our barmen caught some scumbag dosing up a girl's drink from a little plastic bottle like they use for eyedrops. Bouncers held him for the cops. They hauled him off after we took a photograph and hung it up behind the bar and by the street entrance to eighty-six him. Couldn't tell you if there was a trial or what."

"In other words," Blade said, "your place is squeaky clean."

That drew a snort from Connors. "I was born at night but not last night," he scoffed. "Does shit go down that I don't know about? Undoubtedly. Is someone snorting in the john from time to time, or ripping off a quickie in one of the stalls? Could be. State law forbids us putting CCTV in the crappers for security, you know. More lawyers calling us voyeurs and seven other kinds of perverts if we tried that."

"Do you know a Rick Johnson from Staten Island?" Grant inquired.

"Nope. Never heard of him."

"Or anyone named Devon?"

"Customers don't give their names too often. Not to staff, at least, who've got their hands full anyway. Unless it was a chick and she was smokin' hot. That might hit home with some of 'em."

"Rules about dating customers?" Blake asked.

"None of my business if a staffer's off the clock."

"Right. Thanks for your time," Blake said, then dropped a line he'd always hope to try, lifted from movies and TV. "Don't even think of leaving town until we've cleared this up."

The night manager grinned and spread his hands. "Where would I go, man? Everything I need's right here."

Great Kills, Staten Island

Great Kills is the northernmost community on Staten Island's South Shore, fronting on Raritan Bay. Its morbid-sounding name doesn't refer to massacres, but comes down from the ancient Dutch word *kill,* meaning a creek or channel.

Protected by NYPD's 122nd Precinct, the town's forty thousand-some residents break down 88 percent white (including Hispanics), with various people of color comprising the rest, spread out at twenty inhabitants per acre.

Only one of those concerned Reg Hardy and Stan Dartnell today.

Rick Johnson lived in a drab apartment house on Greencroft Avenue, a block from Great Kills Park, part of Staten Island's Gateway National Recreation Area, supervised by the National Park Service. On summer afternoons, if he had left a window open, Johnson might have heard locals and tourists laughing, maybe smelled their barbecue aromas wafting up from designated picnic areas.

Today was overcast and spitting rain in flurries when the SFX commandos rang their subject's cheap doorbell and heard in chime inside. It took a while for Johnson to respond, then the door opened to reveal a young man in his twenties, raccoon rings around his eyes from lack of sleep, unruly hair that needed washing, and an old track suit that likely doubled as pajamas.

"What?" he asked them.

Hardy introduced the pair of them, stated their business. Johnson replied as they'd expected.

"I already gave my statement to all kinds of cops, yo."

"We just need to clear a few things up," Dartnell explained. "Should we come in, or would you rather talk about it on the doorstep with your neighbors listening."

"Starting to think I need a lawyer, yo."

"That's up to you, of course," Hardy replied. "Tell him to visit you on Rikers Island."

"Hey, man—"

"In or out, mate," Dartnell said. "What'll it be?"

"Okay. Come in, already."

The apartment was a pigsty. Hardy didn't like the tenant's odds of getting his deposit back. Said tenant cleared a greasy pizza box, some other fast-food bags and from a thrift store easy chair and sofa, claimed the chair himself and slumped into it while his visitors sat on the sofa, springs gouging their backsides.

"I suppose you're gonna ask me about Devon," Johnson said.

"He's on the list," Hardy agreed.

"You wanna know the truth?"

"It's normally preferred," Dartnell agreed.

"Okay. I only met him just the once, on Saturday. I'm at the bar, drinking Corona, he comes up next to me. Says, 'Hi, I'm Devon. Let me get the next round.' I thought he was gay at first, but free beer's still free beer. No strings, right?"

"You thought he was gay *at first*?" Dartnell inquired. "What changed your mind?"

"No sooner do the beers show up, when he points out a pair of honeys at the far end of the bar. He wants to pull one of 'em, but he's worried about one guy hitting on the pair of them together. Better with a wing man, yo."

"And that was you," said Hardy.

"Roger that. I'm thinking hey, free beer and maybe I can snag a little something-something on the side, you know? He had his eye on the brunette, but who cares, right? There's nothing wrong with blondes in my book."

"So you were backup," Hardy said.

"Yeah, man. Just like I told the other guys with badges."

"How would you describe this Devon?" asked Dartnell.

"Nothing special, Dark hair and about my age. Wearing a short-sleeved shirt and jeans with Dockers."

"Short sleeves," Hardy repeated. "No ink on his arms? Nothing that could identify him?"

"Just a cheap-looking wristwatch. Something you'd find at a drugstore on sale."

"No rings or other jewelry?" asked Dartnell.

"Nothing I say," Johnson replied. "I wasn't looking down his shirt, you understand."

"He wear a belt with those jeans?" Hardy asked.

"Plain leather."

"And the buckle?"

"Hey, now that you mention it. Kind of a cowboy buckle. Not one of the big ones from a rodeo, but squared off, with a scorpion on it. How'd I forget about that, talking to the cops?"

Reg Hardy shrugged. "What kind of metal? Could you say?"

"Silver or stainless steel, I think," said Johnson. "But it had a kinda faded look about it, like that 'stainless' silverware they sell that stains first time you use it? What's the word?"

"Tarnished," Dartnell suggested.

"That's it, yo! And I swear that's all, except…"

"Spill it," Hardy commanded.

"Well, it was the way he looked at Carrie and something he said when we were headed over toward 'em. 'She's mine' and 'bank on it' or 'take it to the bank,' something like that. It sounded weird but what the hell? My mind was on the blonde by then."

Hilton Garden Inn, Manhattan

After their preliminary probes, the team regrouped at lodgings that the FBI had booked on East 33rd Street in Midtown. Three rooms, the men paired off, and one for Karpin in the interests of "propriety." They had convened in Grant and Blake's room after checking it for listening devices.

"Anything new?" Mahoney asked the others.

Hardy spoke up first. "This Devon bloke, assuming that's his name in fact, wore a belt buckle with a scorpion in tarnished silver, maybe stainless steel. Cops don't have that."

"A longshot third material might be pewter," Dartnell chipped in.

"No other jewelry and no identifying marks," Hardy concluded. "But he had a fix on Carrie Maddox going in. Recruited

Johnson to divert the girlfriend while he made his move."

"No idea why?" Blake asked.

"None other than the obvious," Dartnell replied. "He hadn't known his new sidekick ten minutes when he picked her from the crowd. Told Rick, 'She's mine. Bank on it.'"

"Was he acting high?" Grant asked.

"Or borderline stupid," said Hardy. "No one with connected gray matter would drop hints to a financial motive going in."

"But Johnson didn't pick up on it at the time or think about it later, talking to the law."

"He's not the sharpest chisel in the toolbox," Dartnell said. "Took one look at the blonde and started thinking with his little head until it blew up in his face."

"Michelle paid no attention to the belt buckle," said Natalie. "I asked about identifying marks, though, and she came up empty."

"That confirms what Johnson said," Hardy declared. "Young Devon wore short sleeves that night, with no sign of scars, tattoos or any jewelry."

Grant talked to them about their meeting with Brady Connors then. "He has the rap down pat. They card whoever might be underage and wand potential patrons if the bouncers think they might be carrying. Beyond that, state law won't permit them searching anyone for hidden drugs or watching what goes on in either restroom. Yada-yada. Same thing that he's used to telling cops and now the bureau."

"What's your feeling?" Natalie inquired.

"I wouldn't trust him if his tongue came notarized," Blake said.

"Ditto," his brother readily agreed. "He's not above allowing shit to happen on his watch, as long as he's cut in on the returns. As far as this specific instance goes, I couldn't say."

"Somebody needs to have another word with him," Hardy suggested.

"Oh! Let me!" Natalie chirped, using the girlish voice that

sometimes indicated she was teasing.

Not this time.

"We'd need to have him come through that alive," said Hardy.

"Or until he spills his guts, at least," Dartnell amended.

"I'm the very model of restraint," Natalie said.

A couple of her teammates laughed aloud at that, then let it drop.

"First thing," Grant said, "before we come on hard to anyone, we'll need supplies. I've got our guy in Brooklyn lining up equipment."

"Are we tipping off NYPD to that?" Blake asked. "Enlightening the FBI?"

"A double negative," Grant said. "The senator's behind us and he seems to have the others in his pocket. Anyway, it's easier to get forgiveness than permission."

"I had another thought," Blake said.

"Which is…?" his older brother asked.

"The Dark Web. If there *are* commercial snuff films and a market for them, where else would we start to look?"

"It's big on outlawed porn," said Natalie.

"That doesn't cover much these days," Hardy observed.

"Covers enough," she answered back. "All child-related porn, most bestiality, the S&M that's not strictly consensual."

"Point taken," Reg agreed. "You have a way in?" he asked Blake.

"There are a million ways in," Blake replied. "The trick is finding one that serves a given need."

"Okay, then," Grant pronounced. "You start on that. The rest of us will get geared up. Something you've got your heart set on, bro?"

"Anything that suits the team and can't be traced."

"Our contact's specialty," said Grant. "Let's roll."

4

South Brooklyn Marine Terminal

Rocco Conti was a longtime mobster, but he wasn't "made," meaning he'd never been admitted to the Mafia with finger-pricking, solemn oaths and all that jazz.

At forty-five, no one could say that was from lack of trying.

FBI Director Hoover had spent close to forty years denying that the "Maffia" existed in America. When he discovered it at last, under the Kennedys he hated, old J. Edgar was compelled to change its name, calling it "LCN"—linguistic garbling of *la cosa nostra*—while demoting non-Italian mobsters to the lowly status of "associates." Jews, Russians, Irishmen, whoever, since that day they had existed for the bureau only as affiliated gofers for the "made men" of Sicilian heritage.

That hadn't stopped Conti from building up his reputation as an earner on the streets of Gotham, mostly handling cargo thefts, gambling and various "protection" rackets on the Brooklyn waterfront, where he'd been born and raised, if you could call it that. As long as the Mahoney brothers had relied upon him for specific paramilitary hardware in the States, Rocco had always managed to oblige them, with a cheerful smile and one hand out for cash.

Tonight, despite short notice, proved to be no different.

The South Brooklyn Marine Terminal covers close to ninety acres in Brooklyn's Sunset Park industrial district, along the Bay Ridge Channel between 29th and 39th Streets, granting unparalleled access to the country's largest and most affluent consumer marketplace. No one could sway how much the Mob, by any name, ripped off each year from shipping companies, recipients, or workers constantly in hock to bookies, loan sharks and the like, but all official sources readily agreed that take surpassed the GNP of some small nations on the planet.

"You wanted basics, so I got you basics," he was telling the five SFX commandos ranged before the black Ford Transit full-size cargo van, its double backdoors standing open, spilling light onto the asphalt at their feet. "Nothing fancy, okay? But all brand-new and clean. You have to drop it somewhere, just forget about it. No one's tracing anything."

"Let's have a look," Grant said.

"Sure thing."

Conti drew back a tarp as if he were a stage magician proving to an audience of rubes that he'd just made his cute assistant disappear. His free hand made a sweeping pass that would have satisfied a maître d' or head waiter in any first-rate eatery downtown.

"Rifles, you wanted, so I went with the M4s," said Rocco, while his customers examined six identical, jet-black assault carbines, each paired with stacks of magazines and boxes or loose ammunition.

The M4s were shorter, lighter versions of the classic M16 rifle, first introduced to military service at the height of Vietnam's long conflict, back in 1964, updated and supplanted by the M16A2 eighteen years later. The M4 measured 29.7 inches with its collapsible stock retracted, compared to the parent rifle's 39.5 but tied the M16's weight of 7.5 pounds fully loaded. Both fed 5.56×45mm NATO rounds, manufacturers reporting a full-auto cyclic fire rate between 750 and 900 rounds per minute, scaled back to one round per second on semiauto. Globally, at least sixty-six countries issued M4s to their military and/or law enforcement agencies.

When Rocco's customers had all approved the shoulder guns SFX was buying, their supplier moved on to the pistols he'd selected—once again jet-black with "furniture" molded from polymer, each gun supplied with extra magazines and ammo.

"New Glock Model 22s," he said. "Can't beat 'em for dependability, as you well know."

An Austrian product, once falsely labeled "plastic guns" by sloppy journalists who claimed they could defeat airport security devices, the first Glocks had been introduced in 1985 and took the shooting world by storm, diversifying from the original 9×19mm Parabellum Glock 17 into thirty-odd models, with calibers ranging from .22 Long Rifle up to .357 SIG and .45 Glock. The Model 22 chambered .40 S&W ammo, favored for its stopping power by the FBI, NYPD, and other law enforcement agencies worldwide from Canada to the Philippines and Australia. Each standard magazine held fifteen rounds and featured tiny "witness holes" that let a shooter keep track of the rounds expended in a firefight.

Again, the team approved after a cursory examination of the sidearms being offered. Rizzi tossed in holsters for the Glocks, DeSantis Criss-Cross models that accommodated various positioning on belts up to 1.5 inches wide.

"You didn't mention silencers," Conti reminded Grant. "Maybe I should've asked about 'em, but—"

"We shouldn't need them," said. "What's it come to for the lot."

"Just what I quoted on the phone," Rocco replied.

"Okay, then."

Grant handed a roll of fifty-dollar bills to Conti, who would never sell a stick of gum on credit, hadn't cashed a check in twenty years or more, and only handled credit cards if he was forging them. The mobster didn't count the payoff, trusting Grant as much as he had ever trusted anyone, based on their dealings in the past.

"The duffel bags are my treat, folks," he said.

"Appreciate it, Rocco," Grant replied. They shook hands while the other SFX commandos fastened holsters to their belts, seated their Glocks, and stowed the rest before dispersing to their vehicles. The van pulled out before they did, and moments later there was only silence on the pier.

Somewhere

Carrie Maddox woke in darkness with a splitting headache, no idea of where she was or how much time had passed since she's lost consciousness. She tried to move but instantly discovered that her wrists and ankles had been flex-tied, hands secured behind her back.

Don't panic, she advised herself, which didn't help at all.

The pitch-black that surrounded her was absolute, no cracks of light denoting doors or windows anywhere. The chamber, cell, whatever, was unheated, damp, and smelled of mold. Maybe a basement, or some kind or storage space disused for months or years on end. Her brain was fuzzy from whatever had been slipped into her last drink at The Red Zone, but she tried to focus her remaining senses now that vision was denied to her.

First, listening. She heard the sound of water slowly dripping, could have been a leaky pipe or sink that someone had not turned off properly, but judging distance and direction were beyond her at the moment. There was nothing else: no muffled sounds from television, radio or conversation in adjoining rooms; no traffic noise; no flushing of commodes; and—thankfully—no squeaking, scrabbling sounds of rodents on the prowl for food.

Next, smell. Her brain had already absorbed the scent of mold or mildew, but it picked up no suggestion of a furnace running or of kitchen odors. Carrie smelled herself, unfortunately, and determined that she'd wet her pants at some point while unconscious. From the chill of it, she knew that had been sometime back, giving the moistened fabric of her slacks and underpants the opportunity to cool.

Which brought her to the sense of touch.

Aside from wrists and hands securely bound, the clammy wetness at her groin, Carrie knew she was lying on her left side with a thin and lumpy mattress underneath her. Beneath that, a cautious movement of her hobbled feet discovered, lay a concrete floor. The mattress wasn't much, in terms of comfort, but she balked on rolling from it go explore her cell, worried about what she was likely to encounter, maybe something that would fall and add fresh pains to the insistent throbbing in her skull.

Her slacks had pockets, but they had been emptied and turned inside out. The pocket lining on her right side, toward the ceiling that she couldn't see above her, tickled at her forearm. Whoever had drugged her at The Red Zone had removed all personal belongings she was carrying, however long ago she'd been abducted.

That made Carrie think about her father and stepmother, wondering if they were yet aware of what had happened to her. Dad would move Heaven and Earth to help her if he could, employing his considerable resources to that end if he had the opportunity. As for Jolene, they'd never liked each other, though her stepmom tried to hide that fact from Harlan Maddox to the best of her ability.

Another thought intruded now and sent a cold chill racing down her spine. Something her mind had just coughed up to torment her. Daddy would obviously help her *if he had the opportunity*, but if she had been kidnapped by some random psychopath, how would Virginia's senior U.S. senator find out in time to save her? Would he ever know at all, unless her ravaged corpse turned up some day, so badly decomposed that she could only be identified by dental records?

Shit!

You heard about it every day, females kidnapped and slaughtered, some confined as playthings for some pervert, held for years on end in basements, closets, sometimes coffin-sized boxes shoved underneath a madman's bed at home. Some freaks started collections, keeping half a dozen slaves or more concealed from neighbors' prying eyes, only exposed when one escaped by pure dumb luck or their abuser was arrested on some other charge and spilled his guts in custody.

It was a weird, wild world, and there were more nuts on the streets than locked up in asylums.

One freak out in Philadelphia, she thought it was—couldn't recall his name—had kept his captives in a well and fed some the remains of others when he'd knocked one off, providing inspiration for "Buffalo Bill" in *The Silence of the Lambs*.

Art imitating grisly life.

Carrie dispensed with running down the list of gross mistakes she'd made last night. Drinking too much for starters—not unusual of late—and tacking on The Red Zone as a late addition to the list of clubs she visited with her friend, Michelle. Connecting with a pair of shady dudes she never seen before. Not watching closely as the one called Devon handed her the last drink she'd imbibed. Allowing yet another total stranger—that one female—to convey her from the ladies' room under the guise of "helping" her.

Now, here she was, and Carrie's only consolation was that she appeared to be alone. Granted, that scared the hell out of her, but it still could have been worse. Michelle, as far as Carrie knew, was still at liberty and would have sounded the alarm by now.

Whenever *now* was.

Just to verify that point, she tried her voice—raspy—half-whispering, "Michelle? You there?"

Nothing. And that was good, unless…

Don't go there, she advised herself. Nothing had happened to her best friend in the world.

Or, if it had, Carrie guessed she might be as good as dead.

The Majestic, Central Park West

Rank has its privileges, in government as in all other walks of life.

Harlan Maddox owned three residences. One, his home for purposes of voting and assigning federal pork to his constituents, was a plantation outside Richmond that his family had owned from antebellum times down to the present day. Before the Civil War, slaves worked its cottonfields, a task performed today by tenant farmers whose condition varied little from that of their ancestors, despite a grant of voting rights bestowed in 1865 but only realized a century later. His forebearers had been die-hard Democrats until the 1960s, then had switched parties to follow Barry Goldwater and other GOP proponents of "states' rights." Money still talked, whether a politician ranked himself as "blue" or "red."

The second Maddox residence was a midsized house in Washington, D.C.—specifically in Georgetown, where his neighbors were the upper crust of Congress members and associated bureaucrats.

The third, which he'd be occupying until Carrie had been found alive and well, was The Majestic, on Central Park West in Manhattan, where co-ops started at a million dollars plus and soared into the stratosphere from there.

Ex-tenants of the ritzy complex had included entertainers Milton Berle, Zero Mostel, fashion designer Marc Jacobs and celebrity gossip monger Walter Winchell. On the darker side, its occupants had once counted the rancid "cream" of underworld society: Meyer Lansky, Lepke Buchalter, Lucky Luciano, and the Mafia's "prime minister," soft-spoken Frank Costello. TV host Conan O'Brien sold his co-op in 2010, but the remaining residents, while little known away from Wall Street, represented many *Fortune* Top 400 companies.

This evening, while Harlan Maddox sipped his sixth or seventh Lagavulin sixteen-year-old single malt Scotch whisky—ninety dollars for a twenty-five-ounce bottle—wife Jolene sat on the loveseat to his left, a cautious yard of empty space between them.

"Harlan—"

"Don't," he cut her off.

But Jolene Maddox wasn't one to be denied. "You need to hear this," she insisted. "The police and FBI are doing all they can right now. You have to trust them."

"Maybe with somebody else's only child," he said.

That stung, as it was meant to. An abortion during Jolene's movie days had gone awry, and while she campaigned for adoption early in their marriage, Harlan wouldn't budge on his refusal to inherit "someone else's problem" from the human gene pool.

"Besides," he added, while she fumbled silently for a response, "it's gone beyond that now."

"Care to explain that?" she inquired.

"I've employed a group of specialists."

"Private investigators?"

"Not exactly."

"What, then?"

"Never mind. These people get results, or have done in the past, to help our government."

She puzzled over that and didn't like the general direction where that train of thought was leading her.

"You mean, like bounty hunters on TV?"

"You'll never see these people on the tube, Jolene," he said. "The people they go hunting, maybe. Never them."

"I think you've had enough to drink, Harlan," she warned.

"I know my limits," he assured her. "Like I know the FBI's, NYPD's, the whole damned shooting match."

"And what if something should go wrong? What if these amateurs—"

His grating laugh surprised and silenced her. "One thing they're absolutely *not* is amateurs. We have less than a day now to resolve this thing and bring my daughter safely home."

"*Our* daughter," she reminded him.

He shot a sidelong glance at her, drank down his glass of Scotch. Said nothing as he reached for the Lagavulin once again.

Jolene frowned, studying her husband's craggy face. "Surely you don't blame *me* for this? The fact that she refuses to accept me as—"

"Don't be ridiculous," he cut her off. "This isn't about you. These sons of bitches want to clean me out. Maybe they're money-hungry lunatics. Maybe someone standing behind them wants me broken, even out of office. When they're run to ground I'll know."

"So, now it's a conspiracy?"

"Jolene, whenever two or more scumbags collaborate on any crime it's a conspiracy, by definition under law."

She set her empty wine glass down and said, "It feels late, after all that's happened. I'm going to bed. Join me?"

"I'm staying by the phone tonight."

"You know we have one in the bedroom, right?"

"Goodnight," he said, and switched the flatscreen television on with its remote control.

Somewhere

Somebody's prepaid cell phone warbled, answered on the second ring.

"Yeah?"

A distant voice spoke urgently, not loud enough for anyone except the man who'd answered to decipher. He was listening and interjecting questions. "Who? Well, when? You sure about that?" Answers obviously did nothing to put his mind at ease.

At last he said, "Okay. Yeah, right. I hear you." Cutting off the call, he pulled the burner's SIM card and its battery, then broke the phone in half and tossed its severed parts across the room.

Standard procedure for security, a job like this.

"So, who was that?" one of his sidekicks asked.

"*Which* boss?" the third guy queried. "Mister Movies?"

"Nope. The one who set it up."

"Okay," the second member of their trio said. "What's happening?"

"Her old man's going off the reservation," Number One replied.

"What's that supposed to mean?" asked Number Three.

"The feds and local pigs weren't moving fast enough to suit him. Getting nowhere, basically."

"As planned," said Number Two.

"The bad news is that Daddy knows some people who know other people," Number One advised.

"I don't follow you," said Number Three, the slowest of their clique.

"I do," said Number Two. "Some kinda freaking mercs."

"Are you high, man?" asked Number Tree. "Who gives a rat's ass what they're driving?"

"Not *Mercedes*, dipshit," Number Two said scornfully. "I'm talking *mercenaries*."

"Huh? You mean like Rambo?"

"Rambo's movie bullshit," Number One informed him. "Do you ever watch the news, man?"

"Not if I can help it."

"Private military contractors, okay? Feds use 'em when they've got a job too dirty for the government to handle or the voting sheep to swallow if it leaks. Deal-breaking jobs, get it? And now that's us."

"To hell with this, then," Number Three declared. "I say we call up Mister Movies. Roll Plan B and get it over with."

Plan B was slated as a last resort, in case Plan A went so far south there could be no retrieving it. If Daddy Warbucks missed the ransom deadline, then his little darling had a hot date with one of The Butcher's boys, a one-take filming exercise, and they could move it for a bundle on the darkest of black markets. Once word got around the leading lady was an amateur and the only daughter of a stuck-up Senate honcho, bidding should go through the roof. If some collector wanted an exclusive copy for his private stash, the price tag would include at least six zeroes.

"We ain't calling anybody," Number One commanded. "Not yet, anyhow."

"Aw, man—"

"Aw, shut your piehole. This ain't a democracy, in case that slipped your mind."

"So, how long would we have to wait?" asked Number Two.

"Before we pull the pin? At least until the deadline passes. If the old man can't come through..."

"Could be too late by then," whined Number Three. "If he's put shooters on our trail, he won't just call 'em off after we slice and dice the kid."

"You need to worry about one thing at a time," said Number One.

"I am, yo. It's my ass."

"You're worried about someone capping you?"

"Damned straight!"

"So, think about what happens if the people running this show hear that you've gone off the rails. You'd wind up starring in a movie of your own, and not as leading man."

"This was supposed to be an easy gig," said Number Three.

"Is what it is, man. Drop a downer and get used to it."

"Last time I'm pulling any crap like this, I swear to God."

"The payday we've got coming, that's the plan," said Number One.

"Can't spend it if we're dead, yo."

"Everybody dies sometime."

"Big talk. If that's today, I'm comin' back to haunt you like that thing from *Poltergeist*."

"Feel free," said Number One. "But let's collect the money first."

"Somebody ought to check the package," Number Two suggested.

"Since you're volunteering…"

"Shit! Okay, I'll go."

"And 'check' means have a look. Remember that. No touchy-feely or you might end up short-handed."

"Like it matters once the saw's revved up."

"We've got our orders," Number One reminded him. "Delivery 'as found' means just exactly that. You tamper with the merchandise and you *become* the merchandise. *Capisce?*"

"What, you're Italian now?" asked Number Three.

"Nope. But we know some guys who are, and they're all sticklers for obedience. Keep that in mind."

"I hear you."

Rising, Number Two moved toward the kitchen and the basement stairs concealed in what appeared to be a broom closet. He snagged a flashlight from the kitchen counter as he passed and wandered out of sight.

"I'm telling you, this sucks," said Number Three.

"Shut up," said Number One, "and see what's on TV."

5

Midtown Manhattan

Blake got to work on his laptop as soon as he returned to the hotel on East 33rd Street. Probing the Deep Web and the Dark Web was beyond most daily users of the Internet, but Mahoney had compiled enough experience and shortcuts that it didn't take him long.

The "Deep Web" is not terribly mysterious per se. The term—used interchangeably with "Hidden Web" and "Invisible Web," as opposed to the "Surface Web"—simply refers to portions of the World Wide Web whose contents are not indexed by standard computer search engines. Deep Web is masked behind "HTTP" forms, including many common uses such as email, online banking, web forums requiring advance registration, and private or restricted social media pages. Most sources credit computer scientist Michael Bergman with coining the "Deep Web" term in 2001.

Eight years later, *Wired* reporters Andy Greenburg and Kim Zetter noticed shady operators doing business on Freenet—an ostensibly secure peer-to-peer platform for censorship-resistant communication and publishing—and on "darknets," overlay networks that use the Internet but require specific software, configurations, or authorization to access, focused on providing anonymous Internet access and employing high encryption levels (as opposed to Bing, Firefox, Google and Wikipedia, to cite four of countless common examples).

Digging deeper, those reporters and others found that some 43 percent of Dark Web content was "non-illicit," meaning generally innocuous blogs, email, chatrooms, directories and such. Approximately 5 percent allowed whistleblowers to expose their information without fear of corporate and governmental payback on the job or otherwise. Of course, that still left roughly 52 percent of the Dark Web engaged in activities banned by various state or federal statutes. The ever-growing list included drug-dealing; gambling in jurisdictions that ban it; a panoply of fraud ranging from credit card cloning and wholesale identity theft to electronic bank heists; trafficking in guns without resort to licensed dealers; hacking by "black hats" and "white hats" alike; and unregulated trading in virtual currency labeled "bitcoins," ranked with a 2020 exchange rate or one bitcoin to $6,135, handy for tax evasion and other illegal transactions.

By far the largest portion of illicit Dark Net traffic was determined to involve pornography. Hard-core porn, once branded "blue" or "triple-x," had once been banned throughout America, but it had come out of the legal closet in the 1970s and '80s, starting with films like *Deep Throat* and chasing new technology across the years until most local video-rental outlets had special "adults only" sections where almost anything went. As major chains like Blockbuster and DVDXpress surrendered to the Internet, porn moved closer to home, only a mouse-click out of reach for most consumers armed with credit cards.

Various restrictions lingered on, including bans on trafficking in videos of bestiality (which generally fell under statutes restricting cruelty to animals) and child pornography. Under the U.S. Code and various Supreme Court rulings hashed out over time, images of child pornography were legally denied protection by the Constitution's First Amendment, as were sundry crimes involved in making "kiddie" porn—buying, selling or "renting" minors for illicit sex, possession of the filth produced (even by individual "collectors" in suburbia), and so on. To the horror of some civil libertarians, that ban extended even to "artistic" freehand renderings of sex between adults and minors who never existed in fact, and even to some written matter without graphic images. Both state and federal prison sentences upon conviction of such crimes were commonly severe.

Now, Blake presumed that if commercial snuff films did exist in fact, the Dark Web was ideal for advertising and distributing such twisted shit. Recent surveys claimed that 6 percent of Dark Web content offered "violence," a catchall category ranging from "crush videos" of sadists torturing and killing animals to the bizarre case of Canadian porn "star" Luka Magnotta, a closet cannibal who advertised his wish to meet and eat a stranger while live-streaming the event online in 2012. Bizarre as that might sound, Magnotta eventually found a willing victim and proceeded with his ghoulish plan, then, when his appetite was sated, mailed selected leftovers to schools, newspapers, and two major political party head-quarters. Presently serving life without parole in Quebec, Margotta was suspected in other slayings but never faced trial. On the flipside, he "married" fellow incarcerated killer Anthony Jolin in 2020.

Blake began his Dark Web search for snuff and anything related to it with a wary eye, soon weeding out discussion groups that wrangled endlessly about the countless hoax films circulating globally, chased down a dozen fruitless leads as far as he could follow them, and finally pursued one rumor-stream until he struck a semblance of paydirt.

Mahoney called his brother over to the table where he'd been at work for going on two hours now.

"What's up?" Grant asked.

"I've got a name," Blake said.

"How solid?"

"Won't know till we check him out in person."

"What about geography?"

"It tracks," Blake said. "I've got an address for him in the Bronx."

Grant scanned the information on his brother's laptop screen, seemed satisfied.

"Worth looking into, absolutely. I'll collect the others."

"Road trip," Blake told his computer as he shut it down. And smiled.

Kingsbridge, The Bronx

At twenty-seven, Courtney Bennett thought his life was turning out just fine so far. A serious computer geek and closet pedophile, he'd found a way to mix business with pleasure and derive substantial profit from it, while—so far, at least—avoiding any major conflict with the law.

There'd been a teenage bust in high school, granted, when a neighbor caught him messing with her five-year-old. That cost him eighteen months at Horizon Juvenile Center, a "specialized" detention facility in Mott Haven, followed by two years of court-ordered psychiatric counseling that left him "much improved, no further danger to society" according to his doctor's files.

Bullshit.

All counseling had taught Courtney was how to smile and nod, agree with whatever his shrink told him on any given day, pretending that he understood the error of his ways and was resolved to turn his life around if finally released from supervision. New York law required his juvey record to be sealed from prying eyes, including those at One Police Plaza, and that was cool.

Not that he'd learned a thing, in fact, but what the coppers didn't know would never hurt him.

And the next time he went down, if there *was* a next time, Courtney knew he'd never see the light of day again, except through prison bars or from the exercise yard in maximum security.

The simple answer to that problem: don't get caught.

To help with that he banked offshore and lived a modest life in Knightsbridge, a working- and middle-class residential neighborhood on the southwestern edge of Van Cortlandt Park's 1,146 green acres, best known to non-New Yorkers from the opening sequence of director Walter Hill's 1979 gangland fantasy flick *The Warriors*. Knightsbridge itself was less than half the park's size, sharing a population of some thirty thousand with neighboring Spuyten Duyvil.

Bennett had fallen in love with that name at first glance—"Spouting Devil" in Dutch, an ancient reference to strong tidal currents along its coastline, where the Harlem River and the Hudson met—but he'd stopped short of settling there among upper middle class folks, preferring to scale back expectations and hide in plain sight.

Sometimes he hung around the children's playgrounds in Van Cortlandt Park, eyeing the scenery, but Courtney did no active hunting there. Wouldn't be prudent, risking a surrender to temptation that could blow his perfect life out of the water.

Not when his work on the Dark Web for selected partners gave him access to a range of pleasures he had never dared to entertain before.

Who knew, in high school, that he would turn out to be a pedophile *and* necrophiliac?

It was a whole new world, and when you had the right friends keeping you in business…well, the sky was the limit.

Or was that the sewer?

Tomato, to*mah*to.

While he'd skimped a bit on digs, Bennett felt no compulsion about splurging for his ride, a Porsche 718 Cayman GT4. He'd bought it on time, to keep the $99,200 retail price from raising any IRS eyebrows with a straight-across cash payout. Interest would bump it well beyond a hundred grand, but who was counting anyway.

And it was an unrivaled beauty, racing yellow, advertised at "the perfect sports car. For those who would rather ask 'why not?' than 'why?'" Its mid-engine naturally aspirated, water-cooled boxer 6 powerplant generated 414 horsepower, permitting acceleration from zero to sixty in 4.2 seconds, shooting for an official top speed of 188 miles per hour on a graded racetrack. And at the going rate, you'd best believe that it had all the bells and whistles, plus a few most drivers never even thought about.

Tonight, Courtney triple-locked his apartment's front door—nothing incriminating in the flat, but why take chances—and jogged downstairs, thumbing the Porsche's key fob from thirty feet away. Lights blinked, built-in security devices chirped as they unlocked the driver's door, and he was reaching for its handle when a man he'd never seen before stepped up to him from out of nowhere.

"Courtney Bennett?" asked the stranger.

"Never heard of him," he said, squaring his shoulders for a confrontation even though the guy standing in front of him was clearly big and fit enough to kick his relatively scrawny ass around the block.

"Wrong answer," said another voice behind him.

Bennett swung around to find a second stranger glaring at him. There was something in the faces—not fraternal twins, exactly, but enough resemblance there to guess the two men were related.

"What the hell is this about?" asked Courtney, putting on a show of injured innocence.

"We're going for a little ride," the first man to approach him said.

"I don't think so," Bennett replied.

The duo showed him guns, the younger-looking of them warning, "Think again."

Red Hook, Brooklyn

Red Hook has traditionally been a lair of racketeers attracted by rich pickings on the waterfront. The small warehouse, located at the foot of Richards Street, two short blocks from a huge IKEA store, was owned by Rocco Conti through a holding company that operated from a mail drop in Connecticut, paid all its bills and taxes, but conducted no observable business.

From time to time, as on this evening, it was for rent to trusted clientele for whatever they had in mind, from briefly storing contraband, conducting loopy teenage raves, or sweating a reluctant stoolie in a twelve-by-twenty sound-proofed corner room.

Bennett had tried to struggle briefly, back in Knights-bridge, even in the face of two drawn Glocks, and when he regained consciousness, head furiously aching, he discovered that someone had duct-taped him onto a wobbly metal fold-ing chair. The SFX team stood around him in a semicircle, waiting while their prisoner emerged from dreamland and assessed his situation.

"Look," he said, "there's been a terrible mistake."

"You made it," said one of the sluggers who'd abducted him.

"I don't know who you think I am—"

"We know *exactly* who you are, Courtney."

That was the only women in the quintet talking. Bennett blinked at her, as if deciding that she might be foxy if his taste ran much beyond the age of twelve.

"Okay, so that's my name," he said. "What of it?"

"You're the only Courtney Bennett living in the Bronx," a fellow with a British accent said.

"The only one who's done time as a juvenile for child-molesting," said another, with a strong Down Under lilt.

No point objecting that the damned record was sealed unless a judge agreed to open it. His kidnappers had managed to evade the legal nicety, unless...

"Are you guys cops?" he asked. "Because I haven't seen a badge or anything."

"You wish," one of the duo that had carjacked him replied.

"Cops have a book of rules," the woman said. "We're more like you that way."

"I feel insulted now," the Brit chimed in.

"Still gives this snot stain something to anticipate," the Aussie said.

"Hey, now," Bennett put just the right among of pathos in his voice, another trick his shrink had taught him without meaning to. "I want to help you out. I really do, guys, but you need to tell me what you're looking for."

"A line on snuff films," said the older of the pair who'd snatched him up.

For just a second, Courtney worried that his bladder might let go, but he regained control with an effort. "Snuff films?" he said. "That's just an urban myth, right?"

"Not the ones you peddle on the Dark Web," said his younger kidnapper.

"What? Hey, I don't know who you've been talking to, but—"

"We've been reading your poison online," the Brit said. "You go by 'sado666.' That *is* your handle, right, on Cut-a-Bitch.com?"

Just then, Courtney felt like a small turd circling the bottom of a giant toilet bowl, about do disappear from sight for good.

"You run the site," his female captor said. "Don't bother trying to deny it. We can play this one of three ways, as it stands."

Hopeless, Bennett replied, "I'm listening."

"First option, we can hand you to the FBI, its Cybercrime Division, after which you'll be indicted, tried, convicted, and go off to prison for a thousand years or so with cons dying to meet a piece of trash like you."

"Too slow," the Aussie said. "Due process takes forever and a day."

"Plan B," the woman said. "You name the asshole who supplies you with the videos and pays you for your services and we hang onto you until we verify the information."

Bennett noted there was no suggestion of what happened to him after that. He asked, "And what's the third choice?"

"We make our own movie here and now," their seeming leader said. "And you're the star."

Bad choices all around, but if he had to pick one of the three…

"Well, since you put it that way," he replied, "you're looking for a guy named Shorty."

"More than that," the hard-eyed woman said.

"Shorty Báez is all I know him by," said Courtney. "Someone told me he's a Puerto Rican. Personally, I don't think his *mamacita* named him Shorty, but it's all I've ever known to call him by."

"And who runs him?" the Brit inquired.

Bennett tried shrugging, but the coils of silver tape restricted movement. "Beats hell outa me," he said. "This shit's all compartmentalized, you know? One link gets busted in the chain, it's not a zipper sliding up and down. The chain just snaps. Bye-bye. You wanna know who handles Shorty's action only he can tell you."

"How do you contact him?" the Aussie asked.

"I saved his number on my phone."

The woman stepped up to him, drew a pistol, pressed its muzzle tight against the bridge of Bennett's nose until his eyes crossed, losing focus.

"If you're holding something back," she cautioned him, "I'll get a witch in here to read it from your entrails."

"Jesus! Don't! That's all I fucking know!" Tears streaming down his face from his distorted eyes, his shorts and slacks suddenly damp and warm.

"I'd say we've wrung him dry," the woman said, as she stepped back.

"Well, not from where I stand," the Brit observed.

"Might have to hose him down," the Aussie said.

"Or dump him in the river," said the guy who seemed to be in charge.

"No, no, no!" Bennett blurted, pleading. "I cooperated!"

"But you're worthless," said the younger of his kidnappers. "You barely qualify as human, dude."

"I'll change! I swear to God!"

"How does a mad dog change? Somebody has to put it down."

"Just one thing more," the woman said.

"Yes! Anything!"

"What do you know about a young woman named Carrie Maddox who went missing overnight on Saturday?"

Courtney considered lying, but the state that he was in, he couldn't fabricate a story they'd believe. His shoulders slumped again. "I never heard of her," he said.

"The Red Zone?"

"Isn't that a book by Stephen King?"

"Not even close," the woman said, raising her pistol toward his face.

They dumped Bennett into the river after all, still taped up to his chair and anchored with a cinder block twist-tied around one foot. He sank almost without a ripple, as if gladly received below, the upper world happy to see the last of him.

"Had to be done," Grant said, not needing to explain the reasons why.

If Bennett had survived in custody, there was an outside chance that he might wriggle off the hook at trial or during an appeal down range. Before that, he would certainly regale investigators with the details of his kidnapping and third-degree by individuals whose faces he had seen, even if he was short on names.

From there, the dominoes might start to fall. Six VIPs, at least, already knew about the SFX team's efforts on the case at hand, knew their names and faces, where the company was headquartered and could access the files on work it had performed for Uncle Sam on prior occasions.

Only recently, on an excursion to Colombia, they'd taken out a crooked DEA agent aligned with narcotraffickers, plus his top-ranked conspirator, a brigadier general in charge of National Police activity in Medellín. That rough conclusion to a job they'd taken on for DEA headquarters wasn't included in the finalized report that Grant Mahoney had submitted with his billing invoice, and for that omission they could all face life without parole.

To the six feds his team had met with earlier, Mahoney added Jolene Maddox and whoever she might let the operation slip to in her grief, intoxication, or whatever. He doubted the senator would give her any details, but a husband had to say *something* while he was making moves to rescue an abducted child.

So, cleaning house was an imperative, and no more murder to Mahoney's mind, where Bennett was concerned, than taking out a terrorist who hoped to bring the country down by killing innocents at random. If he had to think about it, he would likely rank Bennett below the terrorist—who was, most probably committed to a cause regarded through the twin distorting lenses of religious faith and outlaw politics as something sacrosanct.

With Courtney Bennett and the human garbage he had served, their only motivation was an endless chain of dollar signs.

Grant watched his brother go online again, this time pursuing details on a man called Shorty Báez, formal given name unknown, presumably Hispanic, possibly of Puerto Rican lineage.

There were at least eight thousand people named Báez living in New York City—eight thousand the census takers knew about, that is—and none of them was tagged as Shorty in city directories. A search of Bennett's cell phone indicated that he classified his contacts by initials only, with exactly one of them logged as "S.B." Blake took that number, ran it through an Internet reverse directory, and came up with Diego Báez, resident of Spanish Harlem in Manhattan.

"Stupid of him not to just use burners," Blake observed.

"Most criminals aren't geniuses," Grant said.

"Lucky for us."

"You've got his address there?"

"Locked in. From this, I can't tell if he lives alone."

"Best we can do without a drop-in."

"Right. What will you do about the snuff site?"

Meaning Cut-a-Bitch. Grant seethed, just thinking of it, but he wouldn't let that show.

"Sit on it for right now," he said. "Later, if we get Carrie back, maybe hand details over to the bureau's Cybercrime Division."

"Or swing by," Blake suggested an alternative, "and torch the place. Somebody's stuck inside, too bad."

"Unless there's no 'there' there," Grant said. "Working online, it could be some guy's attic or a string of places spread from coast to coast."

"I'd like to meet the bum in charge, regardless," Blake replied.

"Ditto. But Carrie's the priority, agreed?"

"And getting paid, of course. I hear you."

"Wouldn't hurt to know a friendly U.S. senator."

"You mean another one?"

"The fellow from Nevada's barely starting out."

"Don't sell him short. Got all that gambling juice from Vegas going for him."

"Speaking of going," Grant advised, "it's time we did."

Grant closed his laptop, rose. Said, "Spanish Harlem, here we come."

6

Spanish Harlem, Manhattan

Spanish Harlem is a portion of East Harlem, also called *El Barrio* ("the neighborhood" in English), is one of Gotham's largest predominantly Hispanic communities. Once known as Italian Harlem, it experienced a sea change starting in the 1950s, with most former residents of Italy and Sicily displaced by Puerto Rican immigrants—dubbed "Nuyoricans"—although some of the originals and their descendants linger on.

San Juan native Diego "Shorty" Báez occupied a four-room walkup near the point where West 16th Street meets First Avenue. Because his native island has been owned by the United States since 1898, though never granted formal status as a territory or a state, Báez was not required to seek a green card when he came to Gotham as a nineteen-year-old visitor in spring of 2011, seeking fame and fortune on the fabled streets of gold.

He should have known better, given his homeland's record of invasion, occupation, annexation, economic exploitation and sporadic heavy-handed treatment from authorities in Washington, despite erratic alternating waves of tongue-in-cheek philanthropy over the years. Still, after struggling for a time he'd prospered in the most unlikely field of all.

Filming and screening brutal death.

Because his trade had certain mortal risks attached, Báez enjoyed the company of streetwise bodyguards recruited from the Savage Skulls, a mostly-Puerto Rican gang with a minority of African Americans included, that had thrived in Gotham since its foundation in 1969. Most of its members were drug dealers and extortionist with a sideline in pimping, but their fearsome reputation also qualified them for a role in personal security.

They always carried weapons and were skilled in using them, a fact attested by their clique's impressive body count in turf wars and engagements with police spanning the better part of half a century and counting. Shorty Báez wasn't dumb enough to brief them on the nature of his business nowadays, but if they'd known the Savage Skulls would not have cared, displaying no more human empathy for strangers slain on camera than for the people they had personally murdered, young girls they had hooked on crack and set to whoring, or the stolen pets they used as "bait" to train their fighting dogs.

That was the great thing about being born and raised without a conscience on the mean streets of a city that invited strangers with its golden promises, then stabbed them in the back. After a short while, nothing bothered you and you were good to go, chasing greenbacks through any sewer where a profit could be made from excrement.

Tonight, Shorty was traveling with four Skulls as his entourage, all festooned with tattoos and floating on a haze of weed. That didn't bother him, since his selected bodyguards were seldom mellowed out by drugs, prepared to leap from twitchy to demented psychopathic rage within the time it took to pull a gun or knife.

Benicio Vázquez was their commander, a lieutenant in the Skulls whose knife-scarred visage told you everything there was to know about the twenty-one-year-old. With him were

José Díaz, nineteen; Manuel Arroy, seventeen; and Segundo Nechodoma, fresh from partying to celebrate his sixteenth birthday at the weekend. All were armed with pistols, switch-blades, and whatever else they packed routinely when they hit the streets. Vázquez and Nechodoma both wore knee-length trench coats that concealed an MP5K submachine gun (Vázquez) and a sawed-off shotgun for Segundo.

Add that to the old Beretta 93R automatic Shorty carried, manufactured last in 1993 but still a classic with its switch that changed the pistol's mode of fire from semiautomatic into three-round bursts. To steady it on automatic, the Beretta had a little fold-down foregrip on its trigger guard, which was deliberately oversized to let a shooter hook his left thumb through the ring of steel. It also had a twenty-round extended magazine that fed the 2.6-pound weapon 9×19mm Parabellum ammunition, and Báez had two spare mags stashed in his jacket's inside pockets.

Tonight Shorty and his companions were en route to meet a guy who furnished starlets on occasion for the videos that Báez posted to the Dark Net, sometimes getting off by watching them himself.

Nobody's perfect, right?

Not that the Skulls were meeting Shorty's contact or had any notion of the role he played things beyond the scope of their limited understanding. If they *had* known…well that would have been a problem that required Báez to terminate their services and shop around for other bodyguards.

Lately, Báez and his connection had become involved in something sweeter than their usual, which promised to reward them far more handsomely than they were used to in their roles as middlemen. A bigger payday naturally meant the risks would be increased, but that was always true in life.

Another twenty, maybe thirty minutes, and he would be sitting down with his contact and ironing out some details that would make them both rich men. And taking special care that no one farther up the food chain tried to scarf him down alive.

Shorty was closing on his custom 1964 Chevy Impala fitted with hydraulic lifts that let it bounce as if Báez were driving through an active earthquake zone. The lowrider was Shorty's pride and joy, rebuilt from scrapyard trash into a thing of beauty that had won him trophies from the festivals conducted each year around Halloween and Christmas.

It was one thing that he could be proud of, without any taint of shame.

Still twenty feet from the Impala, Shorty saw five strangers—all *gringos*—emerging from the parking lot's shadows. One of them, male, called out his named.

"Shorty Báez, we need a moment of your time."

"*Chinga tu madres*," he replied. Then, to the Savage Skulls around him, "*¡Mátalos!*"

Before the gangbangers could kill them, though, the strangers had unlimbered automatic rifles and were firing for effect. The first to fall, Vázquez, went down without a peep, his skull exploding, spraying Shorty's face with blood and mangled brains.

Groping to reach his sidearm, Báez couldn't see a thing for all the warm and clotted matter clinging to his face.

Natalie Karpin had not seen a recent photograph of Shorty Báez, making do with an old prison booking mug shot snapped when he was serving eighteen months for income tax evasion, but she didn't think the first man she had killed—half-headless now—was the lowlife they'd come to find.

Ducking down behind the one she'd wasted, masked by flying blood and gray matter from his *amigo*, the next guy in line was reaching for some kind of weapon underneath his jacket, but she didn't want to kill him out of hand, in case he was their primary target.

It wouldn't do, shutting him up for good before they'd had an opportunity to chat.

Of course, that might not be the SFX team's choice.

Three of the four bad *hombres* still upright had guns in hand now and were seeking cover while they laid down rapid fire. Two pistols and a shotgun working, while the fourth guy, making one last swipe to clear his eyes, was hauling out some kind of chunky-looking sidearm from beneath his blood-flecked jacket, breaking toward a Lincoln Continental parked beside a vintage Chevrolet, the last car that remained between him and the street beyond the parking lot.

"We've got a runner!" Karpin called out to the other members of her team and took off in pursuit.

Before she'd covered half a dozen strides, headlights and taillights on the Chevrolet began to flash, its horn blared, and the whole car started bouncing as if a demented troll were bursting through the pavement underneath it. Natalie was half expecting a *narcocorrido* to erupt from its audio speakers, howling at the night, but she was spared from that at least.

The fleeing figure up ahead of her was ducking, weaving, dodging in a close approximation of the Chevy lowrider. His antics foiled Natalie's bid to frame him in her M4 carbine's Aimpoint red dot sight, but that was just a minor irritation since she didn't want to kill him anyway, at least until she found out whether he was Shorty Báez or some hired *sicario* who could not help them track down Carrie Maddox as her time was running out.

Worse than his spastic efforts at evasion, Karpin's runner had his pistol up and swinging toward her as she closed the gap between them. When he fired, a three-round burst spat through the loud night and she dropped behind the leaping Chevrolet, hearing her adversary's bullets drill its windshield and the old car's gaily-painted bodywork.

Upset at missing her, or maybe by the damage he'd inflicted on the car she now surmised was his, the shooter bawled out

Spanish curses, fired another three-round burst of Parabellum slugs, then turned and started sprinting for the nearby street.

Natalie rose, shouldered her carbine, stock extended, and planted the red dot of her Aimpoint squarely on the rippling jacket midway down the runner's spine, between his heaving shoulder blades. From there, she dropped the tiny beacon lower still, nearly convinced now that the gunman must be Shorty Báez in the flesh, unwilling to dispense with him until they'd had some time to chat.

The gunman ran hunched over, making it a tricky shot, but Natalie was good, her combat skills well-honed by long experience. She dropped her aim twelve inches, give or take, and angled slightly toward the target's left, hoping to make a hip shot that would bring him down without immediately proving lethal.

Karpin stroked the M4's trigger, sent a 5.56×45mm NATO FMJ boat-tailed round hurtling toward impact at six-tenths of a mile per second from a range of forty feet or less. It pierced the flapping tail of her intended target's jacket, punched the air out of his lungs, and dropped him face down on the blacktop, sliding for another yard before he came to rest.

The sudden pain was overwhelming, paralyzing. All Báez could do was bare his teeth and wail.

"*¡Maldita sea eso duele!*" Cursing at the agony he felt.

Shorty had heard of old people who fell and broke their hips, some later dying from pneumonia when they couldn't move around, but nothing in his life had made him ready for such crippling misery. He could not stand or even move his legs aside from helpless thrashing on the pavement, scuffing hello out of his Amadeo Testoni antiqued leather Oxfords that had set him back $1,900 and change, tax included.

"*Chingado* rip-off artists!"

Even as he wriggled on the sidewalk, bleeding out and suffering, money still mattered more to Shorty Báez than most any other thing that came to mind.

Except, maybe, staying alive.

He'd lost his 93R pistol when he dropped, but saw it now, barely within arm's reach, and strained to grab it as he heard swift footsteps coming up behind him. Couldn't be one of the Savage Skulls, since all the other shooting had subsided, and he reckoned they were dead by now.

A woman stood above him, same one he had tried and failed to waste a moment earlier. One of her feet, in black Sketchers with white laces, nudged the lost Beretta 93R six critical inches from Báez's fingertips.

"You won't need that," she told him. "But you might need something else, *amigo*. That's a lot of blood you're losing as we speak."

Báez was not without resources, even now. He had three Kunai throwing knives strapped to his left forearm, a nylon sheath inside his jacket's sleeve, a three-piece set its makers called "Expendables," presuming they'd be used and left behind in an emergency. He'd practiced with them, hour upon hour, until he could plant each blade within the ten ring on a man-sized target from a range of twenty feet, but pulling one of them and flinging it before the *puta* but a bullet through his head would be a challenge even if Báez was in the best shape of his life.

Tonight, he wasn't even close.

Instead of going for the knives, he craned his neck, looked back along his broken body, past his Chevrolet as it began to lose momentum in its jerky stationary dance. He looked for any of the Savage Skulls who might be still alive, hoping he'd find the *gringos* down instead, but no such luck.

"Forget about your friends," the woman said. "They're history."

Or grease stains on the asphalt, from what Shorty saw.

"I've got him," she called out to her companions. "He's still breathing but we're running out of time."

As if to emphasize that fact, a distant wail of sirens reached Báez's straining ears. He thought it just might be the first time in his life that he was glad to see *la policía* rolling up in force.

Stalling for time, he asked the harpy who had shot him, "What you want with me, *gringa*?"

Before she could reply, if she intended to, her four companions joined them, standing in a circle around Shorty with their automatic rifles aimed at him.

"Just information. Give it up and you might live to reach the ER trauma unit."

"*¿Que información?*" Still dragging out the precious seconds while his leaking body cooled.

"We can't do this with NYPD breathing down our necks," one of the others with a British accent said.

That served as confirmation for what Shorty knew already. They were hitmen, plus one hitwoman, and that opened a wide world of unpleasant possibilities. Had he offended someone that he worked for while distributing his product to the ultra-kinky masses who demanded it? He wasn't skimming much—at least, no more than customary from a racket based on blood and secrecy—and had been cautious about covering his tracks.

What, then?

"Too bad you didn't just knock on my door instead of going through all this *mierda*. We could sit around, have drinks, and talk like normal people, eh?"

"Normal," another of the gunmen snorted. "That's a laugh, mate."

"Never mind the small talk," said another, one who seemed to be in charge. "We need to get him out of her right now."

"My car's the closest," said the woman, "but he'll make a mess of the upholstery."

"We'll put him in the trunk."

Without further discussion, the four men slung their carbines from shoulder slings and hoisted Shorty off the blood-slick pavement, one gripping each arm of leg. The *gringo* on his left arm felt the sheathed knives, called a halt to the proceedings long enough to snake a hand up Shorty's sleeve and rob him of his last hope that he might survive the night.

That done, they lifted him again, ignoring his pained protests, and proceeded toward the nearest curb. The woman reached a dark sedan ahead of them and popped its trunk. They dropped Báez inside, making him squeal, one of them reaching up to slam the lid.

Before darkness descended on him, one advised, "Keep pressure on that hip. You're no good to us dead."

Harlem River Drive

The Harlem River is an eight-mile tidal straight flowing between the East River and Hudson, separating the island of Manhattan from the Bronx on the New York mainland. The river's northern stretch, called the Spuyten Duyvil Creek, was straightened from its prehistoric curve by excavation of the Harlem River Ship Canal. Six years later, with the start of Prohibition, it became a frequent dumping ground for bootleggers rubbed out by stronger rivals.

And the river still had room for more.

Reg Hardy and Stan Dartnell dragged Shorty Báez from the trunk of Natalie's rented sedan and dropped him near the riverbank, a half mile from the Henry Hudson Bridge. The snuff purveyor grunted when he hit the ground, mouthing a string of Spanish curses, getting zero sympathy from his custodians.

"Still bleeding," Grant Mahoney noted. "That looks bad."

"I need *un hospital*," Báez complained.

"You need to talk," Blake said, correcting him. "Then we'll decide if you're worth saving or you feed the fishes."

"*¿Hablar de qué, hombre?* Talk about what?"

"About the special movies you supply to Courtney Bennett for his website."

"*¿Quien?* I never heard of Corey What's-his-name."

Blake gave the scumbag's wounded hip a none-too-gentle kick, evoked a squeal or pain. Said, "This isn't the smartest time to lie, *amigo*. Bennett gave you up."

"*¡Pinche cabron!* When I get hold of him—"

"You'll need to look for him in Hell, mate," Reg Hardy observed. "He's likely saving you a pew."

Báez blinked rapidly at that, his mind obviously in overdrive behind his beady rodent's eyes.

"You killed him, eh?"

"It wasn't suicide," Blake said. "The question now is, would you rather follow him or take your chances with a jury?"

"Say again about *estas peliculas especiales*, what you call these special movies."

"He's playing with us," Blake said, pulling out his Glock. "I'm gonna cap him."

"No! *¡Espere por favor!*"

"I'll wait ten seconds," Blake informed him. "And my watch runs fast."

"I don't know who makes the movies, *ese*. I can tell you one guy does some of the casting, though. That good enough?"

"We're listening," Grant said.

"You ever hear about a nightclub called *La Zona Roja*, over in Soho?"

Grant and Blake exchanged glances. "The Red Zone, yeah," Blake said, not giving anything away. "So, what about it?"

"There's a dude in charge at night named Brady. Brady Connors, *ese*. Always got his eye out for young talent, Do you feel me?"

"Starting to," Grant said. "Go on."

"He spots these *chicas*, man. The photogenic type, you

know? Maybe a custom job sometimes, or just a certain look that turns him on, eh?"

"And?" Blake prodded him.

"And he makes a call, okay?"

"For what? To grab one of them from the club?" Reg Hardy interjected.

"*Sí,* it happens, man," Báez replied. "But he can't pull that shit too often, right? Only like once a year or so, else he's got cops crawling all over him."

"How does it work the other times?" Natalie asked.

"This guy locks onto one he likes, he's hanging out behind the bar, wise-cracking, flirty-like. Don't matter that he's older. Half the *chicas* go in there are LOA already."

"LOA?" Dartnell queried.

"Yeah, *ese.* Loaded on arrival." Even in his pain, the weasel managed to produce a wheezing laugh.

"And then, what?" Blake demanded.

"He comes up and tells 'em he's the manager and needs to see I.D. before he serves 'em, right? They're flattered, *ese,* wishing they could pass for older even if they're twenty-one. Out comes the driver's license and he looks it over, memorizes the address and all for pickup later, when *la policía* can't connect it to his joint."

"The owners know about this?" Grant asked.

"Nah, man. Brady keeps it on the downlow, like he's skimming from the till but making bigger money, eh? *Mucho dinero, ese.*"

"Who's the buyer?" Blake demanded.

"Man, I don't get into that. Some things are better not to know."

"And you were never curious?" asked Natalie.

"You never heard that old wise tale, *chica*? *La curiosidad mató al gato.*"

"Yeah, I've heard it," she replied. "Except it's 'old *wive's* tale,' not 'wise'."

"Whatever, *mama*. That's all I can tell you, anyways."

Grant looked around at his companions. Asked, "Who buys it?"

Four hands rose. Grant nodded. Still had once more question, though, knowing it was a long shot. "Have you ever heard of Carrie Maddox?"

"Who, *ese?*"

Mahoney spoke the name again, slowly, as if communicating with a mentally defective child. Báez looked blank and shook his head. "No, man. She somebody important?"

"To her family," Natalie said. "To us."

"Wish I could help you, *chica*, but the name means *nada* to me."

"Okay, then," Grant said. "I guess we're done here."

"You can drop me at *el hospital* then, eh? I won't say nothing to the cops, man. *Puedes confiar en mi.*"

"Trust you?" Blake said, smiling. "That's the best joke that I've heard today."

"You think I'd rat you out, *ese*, and burn myself at the same time?"

"I think you are a rat," Blake said. "And New York's got enough of those running around already."

"Hey, man! What about your promise?"

"Anyone remember any promises?" Blake asked the team.

Around the circle, four heads shook from side to side.

"The river, then," Grant said.

Karpin spoke up. "I wouldn't want to drown him," she protested.

"No, you're right," said Blake. "Mercy's my middle name."

His Glock spoke once, its echo rolling off across the Harlem River toward the Bronx.

7

Café Moskva, Brighton Beach, Brooklyn

Situated east of Coney Island, fronting the Atlantic Ocean, Brighton Beach was built around a grand hotel and race-track in the latter 1870s, named for a popular tourist resort in Britain's East Sussex. A fire razed much of the boardwalk in 1919, but promoters built it up again in time to prosper during Prohibition from the Coney Island overflow.

From those days through the Great Depression, first- and second-generation Jewish-Americans flocked to the neighborhood, after World War II by some fifty thousand Holocaust survivors. At the same time, quality of life declined as residents aged out and poverty increased, homes subdivided into single-room apartments for seniors, the poor and mentally ill. The mid-1970s brought a revival thanks to mostly Jewish émigrés from Soviet Russia and Ukraine. So many made that journey that the neighborhood was dubbed "Little Odessa," for Ukraine's port city on the Black Sea.

And with immigrants, as always happened everywhere throughout the course of human history, came crime.

Joel Carmichael III resented being called to Brighton Beach—and Café Moskva in particular—but there was nothing he could do about it. With the wealth he had accumulated over time, descended from a Pennsylvania family once powerful in shipping and railroads, he had accumulated debts, responsibilities, and burdens that would dog him till his dying day.

And how far off that day might be was anybody's guess.

Carmichael had burned through his trust fund in the 1980s, producing derivative low-budget movies such *Beverly High Blowout* and *Satan's Angels,* then segued into hardcore porn in the 1990s, using actors past their prime. When younger stars, directors and producers edged him out of that field, he had gravitated toward a rougher audience, including freaks he personally loathed but who were rich enough to bankroll and enjoy bizarre, sadistic "specialized" productions, and that shift had brought him into contact with the Mob.

Two Mobs, in fact.

First up there was the Mafia, of course, established in New York since sometime in the 1890s and evolving over time until one of its chief accountants quipped that the network banked more per year than U.S. Steel from gambling, drugs and racketeering. The old-line Italian families faced competition in the modern age from Chinese, Japanese, Jamaicans, Cubans, take your pick, and had achieved wary collaboration with the Russian *mafiya,* but Carmichael's original connection with *la cosa nostra* was and still remained a *capo* from the venerable Staten Island Giordano Family, Angelo Rizzo.

Known to friends, NYPD and feds alike by a nickname he'd earned in spades: "The Animal."

They'd started out in snuff together, working with the Café Moskva's owner—though his name appeared nowhere on any deeds or contracts—Shamil Povetkin, aka "The Butcher." Yet another street name earned the hard and bloody way, in Russian lockups and around New York since he had fabricated bogus travel papers, emigrated to the States, and started buying influence with any politician who would play for pay.

And that, it seemed, was most of them.

The three men sat together now in Shamil's private office, sipping Dazbog Russian Roulette coffee spiked with vodka, Carmichael pretending he enjoyed it while the two hardcases seemed not to be faking it. The only snacks on offer were a bag of sweet-corn chips labeled Hukutka and crackers spread with soft and slightly sour Gollandsky cheese.

No matter. Carmichael was not expecting dinner when he walked into the place.

Their topic of discussion—no surprise—was Carrie Maddox and their scheme to squeeze her father for a cool $2.5 million if he ever planned to see his little girl alive again.

Carmichael had not been a party to the kidnapping himself, knew little of such things, although he had been dealing with assorted human traffickers since getting into snuff. Approximately half the "talent" came from overseas, including Eastern Europe, South America and Southeast Asia, where poor families with small regard for daughters readily struck bargains for the brats who didn't pull their weight in sweatshops or by working on the streets. A pittance to the Syndicate might keep a family of slum-dwellers afloat for twelve months, easily. The other one-shot "stars" were homegrown, mostly runaways and adolescent hookers—dignified in PC-speak these days a "sex workers"—who wouldn't make a ripple when they disappeared.

They came from every corner of the country, flocking into Gotham and L.A. with dreams of shaking off their families, striking it rich in front of movie cameras. Funny, Carmichael thought, how when a wish came true it often wasn't as you'd planned, and very few got rich.

Some wound up dead.

Povetkin chomped a handful of corn chips, talking around them as he asked, "How goes it with the senator?"

"He's waiting for a callback," Carmichael replied. "Presumably calling in markers to collect the payoff as demanded."

"Not what I heard," Rizzo said.

"Oh?"

The mafioso shook his head, making his double chins wobble. "Uh-uh. I've got a source inside the bureau."

"Which bureau?" Carmichael asked. "You don't mean…?"

"Right the first time, Rizzo said. "The very same Fidelity, Bravery, Integrity brigade."

"An agent?" asked Povetkin, teeth still gnashing.

"Let's just say fly on the wall at Foley Square and let it go at that," Rizzo replied.

"Okay. And?" Carmichael pressed him.

"There was a meeting this morning," said Rizzo. "The muckety-mucks at the courthouse sat down with a team of outsiders. The senator's call and they couldn't refuse him."

"When you say 'outsiders,' what's that mean?" Povetkin inquired.

"Some bunch from out on the West Coast, works with the feds on quiet, dicey jobs from time to time. Security, I understand. Maybe some wet work on the side."

Carmichael knew what that meant: killing with tacit acceptance from the government, as in Afghanistan, Iraq, and other Third World backwaters.

"You mean like Blackwater or one of those?" the film producer asked.

"I've told ya what I got so far," the mafioso said. "When I hear more, I'll fill ya in."

"Those types don't usually operate inside the States," Carmichael said.

Rizzo shrugged lazily. "What can I tell ta? Circumstances alter cases, right?"

"So are we scrubbing it, or what?"

"We're scrubbing nothing," said Povetkin. "Some toy soldiers try and throw their weight around, we step on them like roaches."

Carmichael experienced a moment's dizziness but managed to pull out of it. "So, then, we're still on track?"

"Damn right," said Rizzo.

Facing them across his desk, the Russian nodded silently.

"All right, then." Rising from his chair, Carmichael said, "I need to make some calls about this. If there's nothing else...?"

"Why don't you run along," said Rizzo. "Keep what I just told ya to yourself."

A side door to Povetkin's office opened after Carmichael had left. A woman entered, crossed the room, and took the chair the film producer had vacated.

"You hear all of that okay?" Povetkin asked.

"The intercom works fine," she said.

"Who thinks we've got another problem now?" Rizzo inquired.

Eyes shifted back and forth. Their new arrival was the first to speak. "I'll work on him," she said. "He's got more backbone that you might think, looking at him."

"And what if you're wrong about that?" asked the Russian.

"Then he goes away."

"About these outside operators," Rizzo said. "Seems like they're making moves already."

"Oh?" Povetkin hoisted one eyebrow. "What moves?"

He had been teethed and weaned on crime, conspiracy, the daily staff of life in Russia under communism first, and now under a semblance of capitalism run by former KGB men and their *bratva* cohorts, *vory v zakone* ("thieves-in-law"), sometimes known as the *russkaya mafiya* or, to law enforcement agencies, more simply as *prestupnaya* ("organized crime"). Thankfully for the several competing syndicates—Russian, Ukrainian, Armenian and Chechen—law enforcement in the former Eastern Bloc was as corrupt as any in the West, if not more so, its honest members commonly demoted, transferred, generally ostracized as rogues.

Povetkin had enlisted with the *bratva* as a teenage thief, muscle, and finally a hitman with a certain style that earned him recognition as "The Butcher." He had been tattooed in prison, serving time for manslaughter and fraud, then immigrated to New York as an ambassador of all that was both highly profitable and unholy. Drugs and weapons, human trafficking, computer hacking into banks and other institutions, contract murders—he had done it all, and with a résumé like that, bankrolling snuff films for perverted clients was only a short step down into a lower level of the cesspool.

Life was good—at least, for him.

The Russian said aloud what Angelo Rizzo was plainly thinking to himself. "Maybe we ought to dump him now?"

"Not yet," the woman said, her voice cold steel. "I said I'll work on him."

"Okay." Povetkin raised his hands, surrendering. "I hope he doesn't let you down, is all. That means he's turned on all of us. We can't allow that."

Telling her that even though she'd planned the snatch originally and they trusted her to see it through, she wasn't bulletproof. If Carmichael lost heart, decided he'd be safer selling out his friends and disappearing into WITSEC under federal protection, someone else would have to pay the price for his inconstancy.

"Don't worry about Joel," she said. "He's putty in my hands."

"The only problem there," Rizzo chimed in, "is putty being soft."

"He knows the price of weaseling out," she told them both.

"All right, then," Rizzo said. "You sold me."

"Fine. Now, I've got people waiting for me, likely wondering what's taking me so long."

"Best not to disappoint them, then," the stocky mafioso said.

Povetkin watched the woman leave as she had entered, through the side door, down a flight of stairs excluded from

the Café Moskva's floorplans, out the back and to her waiting
Cadillac CT6-V sedan.

"Smug bitch," said Rizzo when their guest had gone.

In his world, women had their place and stayed put in it,
whether they were wives and mother, pampered daughters,
gumars that a guy kept on the side, or hookers earning money
for the Outfit on their backs. None of them called the shots
on any business operation, and it raised his hackles that he
had to work with this one, taking guff from her as if she
were in charge.

Scowling, he said, "I'd like to take her out and—"

"When we are finished with her, eh, *moy drug*?" the Russian interrupted him.

From doing business over time, Rizzo knew that *moy drug*
was Russkie for "my friend." He'd also learned *sukinyye* was
"son of a bitch" and *trakhni svoyu mamu* wasn't something
anybody said unless they meant to start a brawl.

"I don't trust her as far as I can toss one of the mansions
that she lives in," Rizzo groused.

"Trust has no part in this," Povetkin said. "The plan was
hers and she depends upon it running smoothly to the end.
As to what *her* end proves to be…well, that is something yet
to be decided, eh?"

"I've got a few ideas," Rizzo replied.

"And I, too. Possibly an accident that will divert attention
from her role in all of this, and more importantly, away from us."

"Fall off a condo balcony, something like that?"

"Who knows, *moy drug*? The world, as we have learned,
is dangerous for reckless fools."

Rizzo allowed himself to smile at that, then let it slip away.

"One problem with the plan, ya know, is pocketing the old
man's payoff without handing back the daughter."

"*Da*. But that was always the intent."

"Don't get me wrong," the mafioso said. "I couldn't give two shits what happens to some snotty college chick, but with her old man being who he is, when the return falls through, you know he'll never let it go. Committees that he's on in Washington, he'll have the FBI, Homeland Security and U.S. Marshals so riled up we'll never hear the end of it."

"In which case," said Povetkin, "certain sacrifices must be made."

"Closing the pipeline?"

"Relocating or suspending operations for a time, at least. Abandoning the industry entirely might be...too extreme."

"And cost us money."

"As you say."

"I know some people we could give up, but I wouldn't trust them not to squeal. Looking at life in prison or the muzzle of some mercenary's gun, they'd absolutely break."

"If they were still alive."

"Now, that's a thought."

"Hansel and Gretel, eh?"

Rizzo could only frown at that. "Say what?"

"The children's story?"

"Yeah, I got that part."

"They leave the breadcrumbs, *da*? To find their way? Before they push the witch into the oven."

"So, we leave a trail to punk the feds, the mercs, whoever, but we clean house in advance and all they find are bodies with the evidence we choose to leave 'em."

"*Imenno tak*," the Russian said, smiling. "Exactly so."

"I like the way you think, Butcher."

Povetkin laughed at that. Replied, "Back at you, Animal."

"The senator still won't give up. You know that, right?"

The Russian shrugged. "He's old. Old men get sick and die. Such things can be arranged."

"It won't be cheap."

"By then we'll have his money and a clean house, eh? Our operation will be up and thriving once again and better than before."

"One thing there'll never be a shortage of is freaks," Rizzo affirmed. "God bless their sorry asses."

"And their deep pockets."

"The best kind."

"Possibly the Maddox girl should wear a mask for her starring performance, eh?" Povetkin asked.

"Why not. Long as she's got no tattoos, scars or birthmarks that show up on camera, the cops can't prove its her. They'll have no DNA to work with, dental records, anything like that."

"And so the FBI can keep repeating that our films and others like them are an urban myth."

"The customers damn sure won't contradict them," Rizzo said.

"I would think not, for their own sake."

"Self-interest works for me."

"We shall proceed as planned, then?"

"With the plan as modified," Rizzo agreed.

"Until tomorrow and the ransom pickup, then."

"Sounds good," the mafioso said, rising to leave. "Seems to me I've got some breadcrumbs ready for the oven."

When Povetkin was alone again at last, he thought about his partners, trying to decide which of them should survive the present situation versus which he should regard as dead wood for the fire.

He had not bothered any of them with the news of Courtney Bennett's disappearance or the incident with Shorty Báez and his retinue of Savage Skulls. There might be more bad news before the sun came up tomorrow, and Povetkin did not want his anymore unnerved than they already were.

Bennett, he took for granted, must be either dead or on the run, afraid to face what happened next. Povetkin cast his vote for death and had already put two of his best *soldaty* on the Internet manipulator's trail to find out which choice proved to be correct. Dead, Bennett could not point a finger back to Brighton Beach. Alive…well, anything was possible if the child-molesting *rastlitel'* faced threats of major prison time.

As for Diego Báez and his men, the raid against them might be mere coincidence, of course. Such things *did* happen, but Povetkin had no faith in them. There were at least a dozen other street gangs in New York that loathed the Skulls—other Hispanics, blacks and neo-Nazis—without caring anything about their sideline covering Báez. But timing was major factor in Povetkin's world, always considered first if no immediate solution to a riddle served itself up on a silver platter.

From corrupt police, the Russian knew that Shorty had not died among his bodyguards in Spanish Harlem, the crime lab people had discovered a large bloodstain separated from the other victims, unaccounted for until their DNA results came back in due time, days or even weeks from now considering the system's workload. In the meantime, Shamil took for granted that Báez had been abducted by the same professionals who's scooped up Courtney Bennett, almost certainly the mercenaries Harlan Maddox had employed to bring his daughter home alive.

Or, failing that, no doubt to punish those involved without resort to courts and statutes that retarded justice rather than advancing it.

Povetkin places his first call to an NYPD sergeant serving the department's Anti-Crime Unit, interrupting dinner with the wife and kiddies, making no apology after the sums he paid the traitor over time. They spoke briefly, his contact readily agreeing to seek information on the Bennett and Báez cases—as if he had a choice. Povetkin would expect an answer first thing in the morning, once his stooge reported to One Police Plaza for work.

A second call reached out to catch a member of the U.S. Attorney's office at an opera performance, forcing her to leave her date, blaming "official business" for the glares from other members of the hoity-toity audience. She claimed to have no knowledge of the Maddox case or anything related to it, but assured Povetkin that she would investigate first thing tomorrow and report back prior to lunch.

So far, so good.

That still left two more calls, alerting cogs in the ongoing operation that their lives might be at risk. Povetkin knew that he was at a disadvantage, warning of a danger from outside that might prove lethal, ignorant or where said threat was coming from or who might be involved.

Offhand, he knew of twenty-six prominent private-sector military contractors with thriving businesses worldwide. Two were headquartered in his native Russia, three more in Peru, Gibraltar and Australia, respectively. By far the greatest number—fifteen—operated globally from bases in America. The U.K. harbored four of major note, and those numbers included only firms that regularly made it into headlines or reports broadcast on television news networks.

How many other were there, that Povetkin did not know about?

He obviously had no clue but *did* know someone who, with any luck, might manage to enlighten him.

A U.S. senator deeply immersed in national security concerns, the military and administration of what he regarded as "justice" would have a list of smaller operations at his fingertips, some of them doubtless willing to involve themselves in tracking criminals where the rewards on offer justified the effort. The problem, as Povetkin realized, would not be laying hands upon that list, but rather winnowing it down, seeking connections to the senator or someone Maddox might depend on at the DOJ.

And then?

The rest would be simplicity itself.

Povetkin's *soldaty* would fall upon them like the wrath of an avenging god. Would chew them up and spit them out again, unrecognizable, like bits of gristle from an otherwise delicious steak.

And with that problem solved, Shamil Povetkin would proceed with life as he'd become accustomed to it since arriving in the States. Compounding wealth, sending the monthly tribute home demanded by his "roof" in Russia—the superiors, *bratva* and government alike, who had entrusted him with managing their interests in New York and environs.

They might not be conscious of the sideline he'd created, but Povetkin knew them well enough to know that they would have no qualms about the market he supplied, the victims it consumed. Assuming they got paid, why should they care?

Povetkin was a long way off from being able to dispense with them just now, but he was working toward that day, counting the months, days, hours until he achieved his goal.

And when that happened, there would be no tribute flowing out of Brighton Beach to pockets in the East.

The cash would all be his, and he would truly be a king.

8

The Red Zone, SoHo

"Didn't I say this guy was hinky?" Blake Mahoney asked.

"You did," his brother granted. "Can you drop it now?"

"Hey, I'm not one to say, 'I told you so'."

Grant laughed at that. "Right, bro. What else have you been doing on the whole ride over here?"

The nine-mile drive from Spanish Harlem to SoHo—mostly south on Broadway, then northwest on Broome Street—had consumed a little over half an hour with red lights and traffic, buses trundling along like dinosaurs, while taxis and impatient private vehicles dodged in and out, pedestrians barging across wherever they felt like it, not a cop in sight.

That last bit was the good news.

Grant supposed that Homicide detectives and their CSI units were busy in *El Barrio,* collecting bodies, playing catch-up to discover who had disappeared after the Savage Skulls went down. He doubted that police were seeking Courtney Bennett yet but wasn't worried much about that either.

At the moment, sitting with his brother, covering The Red Zone while his teammates had the nightclub boxed in all around, Grant mainly worried that they'd wasted precious time reaching this point, about to lay hands on the man who'd probably arranged for Carrie Maddox to be carried off on Saturday.

Would Brady Connors know who gave him orders to proceed? Mahoney had no doubt of that but wasn't sure the guy behind *that* guy would have entrusted Connors with his born identity. A racket like the snuff film trade was fraught with peril up to and including legal execution and elimination by superiors who doubted their subordinates' ability to keep a secret when the heat was on.

And it was on right now.

The good news: Diego Báez had no opportunity to warn his masters between his abduction by the SFX team and consignment to the murky Harlem River. Someone farther up the food chain might well realize that he was missing, but they'd have to open an investigation of their own to find out why, who was involved.

The not-so-good news: If Diego's boss or bosses got the shakes, they might decide to scrub the Maddox operation without waiting to collect the ransom they'd demanded. In that case, their first step had to be eliminating Carrie Maddox, likely getting rid of her so thoroughly—a furnace, maybe, or a burial at sea—that no forensic traces of her would remain for crime scene techs to locate, analyze, and someday talk about in court, before a judge and jury.

Making someone disappear today was no more difficult than it had been a hundred or two hundred years ago. In fact, Grant reckoned it was easier. Americans today, particularly in big cities like New York, Chicago and L.A., paid less attention to their neighbors and events surrounding them than back in 1920, much less 1820. Social media might let them haunt a total stranger's life, track where they dined, who with, and if the meal was great or horrible, but most urban Americans would draw a blank if asked about their next-door neighbors, much less total strangers in a bar or passing on the street.

Maybe a misfit couple ranted in their digs, complaints uncomfortably audible beyond thin walls. Maybe their bed-springs squeaked lasciviously at the oddest times, but that was very different from knowing who and what they truly were.

Grant checked his watch and saw that it was closing time. He keyed his walkie-talkie, told his colleagues stationed all around the club, "Heads up. He could be leaving anytime."

The other three acknowledged him with monosyllables, then cut the link.

Another ten minutes slipped by, and then fifteen. Grant tried to guess what closing chores Connors would handle on his own, which he would delegate to underlings, and which would fall upon the morning crew. It got him nowhere, and he watched The Red Zone's main street exit, wishing that he didn't feel so fidgety.

Each passing moment meant a whittling down of life for Carrie Maddox wherever she was.

Assuming she was even still alive.

Two club employees left over the next half hour but there was no sign of Brady Connors yet, no signal from the other SFX team members that he'd slipped out through a back or side door.

"Screw it," Grant told Blake at last. "Let's go."

He warned the other three, advising them to hold positions, ready at a moment's notice if the whole thing fell apart.

The brothers left their rented car and locked it, crossed the street and tried The Red Zone's door. It opened readily, a fifty-fifty shot since the last worker who'd departed had not stopped to lock it from outside. The fifty-fifty bit was Connors following the last man out, to lock the door internally while he went back to paperwork or whatever, before he headed home.

Instead, the brothers found him lounging at the bar, smoking and talking to a man they hadn't seen before, a bouncer by the look of him, a Mohawk bristling from his otherwise clean scalp.

Connors glanced over, saw them coming. Tried to keep his voice even as he said, "You again? I told you everything—"

He saw the pistols in their hands then and shut up. The bouncer turned, squared off, considering his odds if he rushed the intruders.

"Think about it," Blake advised him. "That would be the worst idea you ever had."

"You got no idea what I think about," the bouncer said.

"I know thinking's a damn sight harder when you're dead."

The bouncer thought about that for a second and was snarling like a wildcat when he made his move.

At first, Brady Connors thought his Mohawk muscle, Skeeter, planned on rushing at the guns, buying his boss just time enough, with any luck, to duck out through the back. Instead, though, Skeeter spun around and threw himself across the bar, dropped out of sight just long enough to grab the sawed-off shotgun racked down there and pop up with it in his hands, jacking a buckshot round into the chamber.

And a lot of good it did him, as the two men who'd interrogated Connors earlier that day squeezed off one single shot apiece, punching the bouncer backwards, falling out of view again and landing solidly on gray linoleum, the twelve-gauge clattering out of his grasp.

Screw this!

The Red Zone's night manager bolted anyway, knowing the triggermen might shoot in him the back but choosing that over a session where they started grilling him by any means that their imaginations could devise. They had to kill him now, since he'd seen them dispose of Skeeter in his bid for self-defense, using a licensed gun.

These guys weren't cops, not even close, logic told Connors that they would no more leave a witness who could testify against them than they would morph into mice and drive a pumpkin carriage to a fairy ball from Mother Goose.

He made it halfway to the beaded curtain screening access from The Red Zone's showroom to a maze of private rooms in back: lockers, storage, employee restrooms, and the manager's office he shared with Ira Greenbaum working days. The backdoor opened on an alleyway, Brady's Chevy Camaro ZL1 coupe waiting for him there.

He'd *nearly* made it to the curtain, when a woman, empty-handed, blocked his path. She was a stranger, no one that he'd ever seen before, but since she wasn't strapped he made the choice to run her down, smash past her, hoping that her presence would prevent his other enemies from firing at him in the doorway and beyond.

And that was when Brady's plan ran out of steam.

He didn't actually see the woman strike a fighting pose but knew she must have, as her open hands, stiffened like cleaver blades, began to hack away at him, accompanied by elbows and a well-placed rising knee.

The chops connected with his collar bone on either side, snapping the shaft on his left-hand side and leaving that arm useless to him. At the same time, an elbow impacted on his nose, flattened the cartilage, releasing spouts of blood from both nostrils. Her knee turned out to be the coup de gras, crushing his genitals, igniting fireworks in his skull, driving the breath out of his lungs.

The next thing Connors knew, he'd dropped into a fetal curl, knees raised to shield his jewels from any further harm. The eerie keening sound he heard was coming from his own strained vocal cords.

His vision cleared by slow degrees, a world of pain descending over him from head to groin, and now he was surrounded by five enemies, all holding guns. Their faces told Brady that he wasn't suffering quintuple vision. These were five distinct opponents, only one of them female.

And she had been the one to bring him down.

"Are we clear now?" one of the guys who'd wasted Skeeter

asked him.

Connors tried to speak but choked on it the first time. Cleared his throat, a raspy sound like sandpaper, and tried again.

"Clear. Right." Taking a chance, he said, "I still don't know—"

A sharp toe struck his lower back, above one kidney, forcing him to squeal again.

"No time for bollocks, mate," one of the men informed him. "You've already lost yours, anyway."

"What. Do. You. Want?"

"We know you lied to us last time around," said one of Skeeter's slayers. "Shorty Báez gave you up. Went on and on about the kidnappings that you've arranged. Before we let you rest in peace we need more names."

Brady didn't like that *rest in peace* remark but tried to stall for time, no clue what he might gain from that or how he could escape from his predicament.

"What names?" he wheezed.

"You're obviously not the brains behind this operation," said the woman who had damn near crippled him. "You have a boss. *He* has a boss. The more you spill, the more likely it is that you'll survive tonight."

Bullshit, thought Connors. He had seen five faces now, his adversaries making no attempt to mask them. Why? Because they didn't plan on leaving him in any shape to talk when they walked out.

"My boss?" he said.

Thinking, *Okay. Why not?*

To put the ball in play, he said, "It's not safe, talking here."

Café Moskva, Brighton Beach

Shamil Povetkin listened to The Red Zone's telephone ring five, six, seven times with no response, then cut the link and tried again. Same frustrating result.

Povetkin checked his Rolex Oyster Perpetual watch and confirmed that the club should be closed, its manager and cleanup crew preparing for departure now. Brady Connors was fanatical about accepting phone calls, but if he had left the club by now...

Povetkin tried his cell, his employee's recorded voice telling him, "I can't take your call right now, but leave a message at the tone or text me. *Ciao*."

The *avtorityet*—ranked as an "authority" or brigadier among *bratva*—cursed the recording. He was not accustomed to such disrespect from underlings and would be sure to punish it when he had time.

That is, if Connors was alive to take his bitter medicine.

If he was not...

That prospect sent a fleeting chill down Shamil's back. If enemies had taken Connors, that meant three so far in one night, with surprising speed. Povetkin reached into his upper right-hand desk drawer and removed the Colt Delta Elite pistol he kept concealed there. The Delta Elite was chambered for 10mm Auto rounds once favored by the FBI before they switched to .40 S&W, holding eight rounds in its magazine with one snug in the chamber. Almost as an afterthought, he took a spare mag from the drawer and set it close beside the Colt.

Even in a secure location, Shamil knew it never hurt to be prepared.

He dialed another number, got an answer on the third ring that time, hearing party noises in the background. When his lackey on the other end stopped laughing long enough to recognize his master's voice, he muttered an apology, excused himself, and hastened to another room where he could shut the door and minimize chaotic background racket.

"Yes, sir! May I help you?"

"Are you celebrating something?" asked Povetkin.

"Only life, sir. Just a few friends stopping over as it happens."

"And how much *kokain* have you stuffed up your nose tonight, when you should have your wits about you?"

"Sir? Only a line or two, I promise you."

"Hear me and listen well. Order your sponging guests to leave right now. Do not explain. Answer no questions. Are we clear so far?"

"Yes, sir!"

"I hope so, since your very life depends on it."

"At once, sir!"

"No. First hear me out. When they are gone and you're alone— none of your *shlyukhi* hiding in the bedroom—you will call the people watching over Carrie Maddox. Do you understand?"

"Yes, sir. And tell them what?"

"That we have come under attack tonight and they must be on guard."

"Attack, sir?"

"We have lost at least one man so far. Two others out of contact may be gone as well."

"When you say 'gone'…"

"Deceased. Stop interrupting me!"

"Yes, sir!"

"The senator apparently has mercenaries on retainer, hoping they can beat the clock and save himself from losing money. He and they will fail, but in the meantime, make the call as I've instructed and report back whatever you learn. Not on your home phone. Use one of the burners."

"Yes, sir."

"Go, now. Throw those leeches out and make damned sure that none of them suspects a thing."

Povetkin cut the link, mindful of how long he'd been on the line. He tried once more for Brady Connors—still no pickup— and then dialed his chief *soldat*, dispatching men to The Red Zone on high alert, to find out whether anything was wrong.

Tonight, he thought, was swiftly turning into *der'mo*, heaps of it, but he was still determined to redeem the master plan, as foolish as it might have been. Povetkin had allowed himself to fall in with the scheme against his better judgment, unable to pass on $2.5 million when it was offered to him and regretting that was no use to him now.

He would find some way to survive the operation and its outcome, even if it fell apart. Let Rizzo and the rest go down for life if necessary. Shamil could escape back to his homeland if it came to that, and in the present circumstances—with the state of agitation between Russia and America, his friends who kept a "roof" over his head—Povetkin had no fear of being extradited from the other side for trial.

And someday later, with a new name, possibly another face, he would return to Brighton Beach and start again.

Shore Boulevard, Brooklyn

Back to the water, this time Sheepshead Bay, with open access to the North Atlantic. Tidal flow would carry any corpses dumped into the bay eastward and bound for Europe till they were discovered by some fishing trawler or consumed by sharks.

In either case, before the stiff snagged in a net or wound up being torn apart, no useful evidence would linger for police to analyze.

When Mother Nature cleans a scene, she does it right.

Eyeing the water underneath a bright three-quarter moon, Brady Connors assessed his chances and decided that he only had one hope—a slim one—or emerging from his grim predicament alive.

His captors weren't afraid of killing. They had proved that at The Red Zone, and he cherished no illusion that they gave a damn whether he lived or died. If anything, they'd probably prefer him dead, unable to rebound and testify against them down the road.

Not that he would, of course—could not, without inviting trial on murder charges and a life sentence at Sing Sing, or perhaps lethal injection by the feds at supermax in Terre Haute. Whether his charges wound up being state or federal, Connors knew he was up shit creek without an oar. Granted, New York had closed death row back in 2008 and had been quarreling over abolition of capital punishment since 2018, but the U.S. government had no such qualms about putting condemned felons to sleep. Presently, sixty-two federal inmates faced execution, sixty-one men and one woman (who'd killed a pregnant mother and carved the fetus from her stomach, claiming that she'd given birth to it herself).

All stood convicted of aggravated murder, and it didn't get any more aggravated than grinding out snuff films to profit from cowardly freaks who lacked adequate courage to kill on their own. It had been sixteen years and counting since the feds last executed anyone, but with the current White House making noise about "accelerated justice," who knew what might happen next?

If Connors played along with his abductors, spilled his guts—no pun intended, thanks—at least he had a slight chance of surviving to witness another sunrise. After that, if he was still breathing, then he could worry about those he had betrayed and the determined hitmen they'd be sending after him.

"So, Carrie Maddox," said one of the men who'd blown Skeeter away back at the club.

"Okay, you got me," Connors said, seated on dirt, surrounded by his kidnappers. "I wasn't straight with you the first time."

"Or with the police," the woman who had kicked his ass observed.

"Well, obviously. Who plays straight with cops?"

"You're wasting time," said Skeeter's other triggerman. "And you don't have much left."

"I'm trying to be helpful here," Brady replied.

"Try harder." That suggestion from the shooter with the British accent, very Michael Caine.

"And keep it simple," said the Aussie. "Tell us where to find her."

"That's a problem," Connors answered. "I don't wanna piss you off, God knows, but the truth is, I don't know where she's at."

"So, you're worth nothing to us, then." The younger of the guys who'd wasted Skeeter raised his Glock, sighting on Brady's face.

"Hold on a second!"

"Time's up."

"I don't have an address for you. That's so I can't let it slip by accident, you dig? I know who's got her, though. We talk by phone. I'm guessing you can trace 'em that way."

"Anybody buying this?" the woman asked her pals.

"I'm being straight with you right now, I swear to God." Connors hope that his attitude impressed them all enough to buy more time. In fact, for once, he was telling the truth.

The fail-safe plan had been Shamil Povetkin's brainstorm, what he called a "double-blind" to beef up their security after they'd snatched a senator's offspring.

"Names, then," the older, slightly taller one of Skeeter's executioners demanded. "And whatever phone numbers you use."

"One more strike and you're out," his maybe-brother said.

"The guy who pulled her from The Zone is Eddie Rattigan. Likes calling himself 'Devon,' but I couldn't tell you why. His sidekick's Mexican, Tony Gutierrez."

"Short for Anthony?" the woman asked.

Brady allowed himself a shrug. "Can't say. I never cared enough to ask him and we don't exactly socialize, you know?"

"Too good for them, are you?" the Aussie asked, sneering.

"Hey, I don't judge, man. We're just into different things is all."

"Except for killing women," said the brunette ass-kicker. "You all like that, right?"

"I like money," Connors said. "It makes the world go 'round."

"Phone numbers," Skeeter's elder triggerman demanded.

Connors reeled them off from memory. Repeated them while one of his abductors wrote them down, the others seeming satisfied to hear them twice.

"And that's all of it?" asked the woman.

"I'm tapped out," said Connors in reply, then let a sly smile twitch around the corners of his mouth. "I mean, unless you want the film director's name."

9

Ozone Park, Queens

Aaron Yablonsky loved two things above all else: money and gambling for more. Given the twin obsessions of his life, he could not have selected a more perfect residence in Gotham than his home on Bristol Avenue in Ozone Park

Founded as "Centreville" in the 1840s, Ozone Park had changed its name four decades later, as one civic planner confessed, to "lure buyers with the idea of refreshing breezes blowing in from the Atlantic Ocean to a park-like community." Today it covered less than one square mile, wherein some 21,000 citizens lived and mostly commuted to work.

Yablonsky's main attraction to the little town was its proximity to Aqueduct Racetrack, the only horse track within New York City's limits, where thoroughbreds ran daily from late October through April. When the horses departed, gamblers still had round-the-clock access to the Resorts World Casino next door, opened in 2011, the first and still only legal casino located in Gotham's five boroughs.

As much as Yablonsky loved gambling, his luck was sporadic at best. His real money came from directing movies, although nothing that would ever grace a local cineplex. He'd started in Chicago, filming hardcore porn for Mob distributors, then served two years at Joliet Prison for hiring underage actors. By the time he was paroled, amateur directors and producers had swarmed the smut market, taking it direct to video, and Aaron had discovered that his slightly higher "standards" were passé.

No sweat.

He'd seen a gap and filled it after moving to New York. "Child-lovers" needed entertainment, too, and it the legal risks involved were vastly greater...well, so were the profits. He peddled his wares to members of NAMBLA—the North American Man/Boy Love Association—and the smaller René Guyon Society, with its slogan of "Sex by eight or else it's too late," then went international with help from connected purveyors, logging sales from Scandinavia and Europe to Australia (AMBLA). Finally, after his second inconclusive interview by FBI agents, Yablonsky saw the light again and looked around for something new.

That downward spiral drew him irresistibly to snuff.

It wasn't Aaron's thing per se, but what the hell? No one would miss the one-film "stars" who came to him through underworld outlets—no one Yablonsky cared about, at least—and just as kiddie porn earned more than "straight" sex films, albeit from a smaller audience, so profits made from snuff were through the roof.

Yablonsky leased abandoned houses, sometimes old clapped-out motels on a forgotten rural highway, and produced as many thirty-minute features as he could before his spider-sense alerted him to danger and he had to split. A flash fire wiped out any evidence that might incriminate Yablonsky or his crew, unlucky actors were disposed of in creative ways that left no trace, and Aaron moved on to his next shooting location down the line.

All good—at least for him, his backers, and the freaks who paid top dollar for a half-hour excursion through the lower depths of Hell on Earth.

Any disturbance to his so-called conscience?

No one ever asked that question in his world, but if they had, Yablonsky might have quoted Leonard Cohen's song "The Future": *When they said repent, repent, I wonder what they meant.*

The difference being that Yablonsky didn't care. Whatever put cash money in his pocket and his offshore bank account was A-OK with him.

Tonight, Aaron was on his way to Resorts World when Shamil Povetkin reached out to advise him of possible trouble impending. It was the Carrie Maddox, thing, of course—a dumb, half-assed idea, Yablonsky could have told his backers if they'd bothered asking him beforehand—and Povetkin had instructed him to wait at home instead of going out. A couple of Shamil's soldiers were coming over and would drive him to a safe house for the next few days, until the mess blew over.

Great. Except that now Aaron was having second thoughts about protective custody.

What it Povetkin didn't plan on helping him at all, but had decided that Yablonsky was expendable, more dangerous alive than dead? A thirty-five-cent bullet could "protect" him from arrest, all right, and at the same time help secure Povetkin against prosecution by the feds down range.

The very nature of their business model proved that life was cheap, and Aaron had no reason to believe he was untouchable, by any means.

So he was getting out, hell yes, but going on his own. He'd grabbed the go-bag that he always kept on standby: containing three passports, prescription meds, four mix-and-match outfits, plus twenty grand in cash and traveler's checks. The pistol in his jacket's right-hand pocket was a Beretta 70, .380 ACP, with eight rounds in its magazine.

Now, all he had to do was—

Ding-dong.

Yablonsky cursed the doorbell's chime that meant he was

too late. Shifting the g-bag to his left hand, pistol-ready with his right, he bent to press one eye against his front door's peephole, wondering if he'd survive the next few seconds.

"Looks like he's having company," Blake told his brother, who was piloting their rented car.

"Could be somebody tipped him off."

They had already double-checked Aaron Yablonsky's address—no mistake—and there were two guys standing at his door at his door on Bristol Avenue, one pressing the doorbell. Out front, against the curb, two others occupied the front seats of a Lexus IS compact executive car, streetlights reflected from its jet-black paintjob. Both were staring at Yablonsky's porch waiting to see if their companions were admitted to the house.

"Smells fishy," Blake said. "Would they send four guys to see if he was safe?"

"More like to make sure *they* were safe," Grant said. He raised a walkie talkie to his lips and told the other SFX team members, "Someone's here ahead of us. Could be an escort or a hit team."

"Either way," Natalie answered back through static whispers, "we can't let him get away."

"Agreed," Grant said. He caught a nod from Blake and told the crew, "We're moving in. Stan, hang out where you are in case our rabbit makes a run for it."

Dartnell was staked out in an alleyway behind the homes on Bristol Avenue, where garbage pickup was accomplished without trucks creeping along the street out front. He had eyes on a redwood fence back there, prepared to intercept the snuff director if he tried to slip away unseen. Hardy and Natalie were parked a block away in each direction, east and west of where the two Mahoney brothers sat and ready to close in as backup now.

"How do you want to play it, bro?" Blake asked.

Grant only saw two ways to go. They couldn't reach Yablonsky's house without passing the Lexus first, which meant they had to neutralize its occupants. Examining the two already on his doorstep, it was obvious they weren't Jehovah's Witnesses out peddling copies of *The Watchtower.* Their coats were too much for the warmish evening, meaning they covered up offensive hardware worn in shoulder slings or fastened onto belts. They weren't police, but as to nationality or gang affiliation, all Grant saw was that they weren't black, Asian or Hispanic.

In New York today, that still left too damned many gangland possibilities.

"They move on us," he said, "we have to take them out. Done deal."

"Okay, then."

When the brothers exited their rental ride, parked catty-corner down the street, they saw the Lexus driver taking note and elbowing his shotgun rider. Both of them could read the situation loud and clear, although the brothers might have been plainclothes police.

Apparently, the lookouts didn't care.

They stepped out of the Lexus simultaneously, one whistling to draw attention from their buddies on Yablonsky's porch. Both passengers were drawing sidearms, but the two Mahoney brothers had their Glocks in hand and rising, sighting quickly from a range of thirty feet or less.

Two shots rang out, the Lexus driver doubling over and collapsing on the pavement, while his sidekick spun away from impact of a shoulder wound and brought his own pistol to bear. Both brothers fired again, in unison, and put him down behind the car, no longer visible on their approach but gravely wounded if he wasn't dead before he hit the curb.

And that left two.

Instead of fighting where they stood, beneath a yellow porchlight, one of the nocturnal doorbell-ringers slammed a flying kick into Aaron Yablonsky's door and burst it open with a crash. Both rushed inside and tried to slam the damaged door behind them, but its locks were shattered and defeated an attempt to jam it shut.

Each jogging in a combat crouch, the brothers separated, crossing a well-tended lawn, advancing on the house. Behind them, they heard Natalie and Stan Dartnell arriving on the scene and leaping from their cars to join the fight.

Along the street, more lights were going on in other homes. Grant knew they didn't have much time before somebody at NYPD's 106th Precinct began receiving calls about shots fired on Bristol Avenue. The cops might have a cruiser in the area by chance, but otherwise, their minimum response time from the stationhouse on 101st Street would be fourteen minutes minimum, with lights and sirens.

Still no time to waste.

Drawing closer to Yablonsky's porch, Grant took a chance. Shouted to anyone inside the house, "Aaron, they've come to kill you! We can help!"

Not necessarily the truth, but passable under the circumstances.

Grant and Blake were almost to the porch when someone smashed a window to the left of their intended target's door and poked an arm out through the flapping drapes, firing two unarmed pistol shots into the yard.

Grant flattened on the grass while Blake did likewise, twenty feet off to his right.

They didn't dare return fired toward the house, for fear of taking out Yablonsky accidentally. The flipside of that coin was that if the intruders really *were* intent on killing him, they could have done the job first thing and cut off any hope the SFX team had of finding out where Carrie Maddox was confined by her abductors from The Red Zone.

Either way, they stood a decent chance of being screwed.

Grant palmed his walkie-talkie, thumbed the button to TRANSMIT, and reached out to Dartnell.

"Stan, if you've got a way to come in through the back, this is the time!"

Ivan Sakharov, inevitably dubbed "The Terrible" by his compatriots, was chief enforcer for Shamil Povetkin's *bratva* family. They had served time together in the Gulag prior to emigrating and establishing themselves in Brighton Beach and citywide. As best he could remember, Sakharaov had murdered twenty-seven people and had thought tonight would make that tally twenty-eight, but it was swiftly going down the toilet now.

Who were the *sukiny deti* who had interrupted his attempt to bag Aaron Yablonsky for his boss? Ivan had no idea and didn't care. It only mattered that they'd killed or incapacitated two of his *soldaty* and now had him trapped inside Yablonsky's house with the snuff film director. Ivan couldn't even call his boss and ask for help, thereby revealing that he'd botched a relatively simple job.

He'd have to solve that problem on his own, with no one left to help but Pavel Yegorov, now that his other men were down and out. And since they had expected no serious opposition from Yablonsky, they were only armed with pistols, nothing heavier, and only four spare magazines between them.

Der'mo!

Ivan's sidearm was a Browning Hi-Power BDA chambered in 9×19mm Parabellum with a fourteen-round magazine and one round in the chamber. Pavel's pistol was a Russian-made Arsenal Firearms Strike One, same caliber and magazine capacity. Between them, prior to Pavel's wasting two rounds seconds earlier, they'd had a total of 104 rounds—ample for escape from any normal situation, not so good if stinking *politsiya* were approaching in response to telephone reports from neighbors.

Any time now, Sakharov assumed.

If nothing else, he must dispose of his intended target first, they worry about enemies outside the house and those who had not reached it yet. Turning, he found Aaron Yablonsky aiming a small pistol at him in a loosed two-handed grip. Those hands were trembling visibly, the weapon's muzzle wavering.

"Pavel!"

Yegorov turned in answer to his name and as he moved Yablonsky tried to cover both intruders in his living room at once. It was beyond him, a pretend tough guy who'd obviously never practiced with the sidearm he was carrying, much less killing two armed men ready to defend themselves.

Instead of firing instantly, Sakharov asked Yablonsky, "What are you doing?"

The snuff director echoed Ivan's question. "What are *you* doing? Why are you here, and who is that outside?"

"The enemy," Ivan replied. "You've had a warning from your *avtoritet, da?*"

"Povetkin called me, yes."

"And then he sent us here to help you. To protect you."

"But he told me no such thing."

"There wasn't time," Sakharov said. "Now put that thing away and let us take you out of—"

"No!" Yablonsky cut him off. "You get out! Now!"

"With murderers outside? Are you insane, Aaron?"

"I'd have to be, if I went out with you."

Sakharov felt the plan slipping between his fingers, lost beyond recall. "*Idi trakhni svoyu mat!*" he cursed and squeezed his Browning's double action trigger at a range of fifteen feet.

It should have been an east kill, but at the same instant, incredibly, Yablonsky shot him in the left shoulder, then half turned and fired off a second shot at Pavel Yegorov. The shots were deafening in Aaron's living room, but Ivan heard a door crash open somewhere farther back, maybe the kitchen, and another man he couldn't see was bellowing in English, "Drop the bloody guns!"

Losing his balance as he recoiled from the jolt of being wounded, Ivan felt himself starting to fall. He still maintained enough control to take another shot at Aaron, striking him low down this time, above his beltline on the left. Yablonsky yelped, lurched backward, triggering another shot toward Ivan as be toppled to the beige carpet beneath their feet.

Behind him, coming into frame now from the dining room, a stranger with an automatic rifle ducked and dodged, tracking the tableau with his weapon, as if trying to decide which target should receive attention first.

Sakharov made that grim decision for him, rapid-riding with his Browning as he fell, until his backside struck the floor—Yablonsky's carpet offering no comfort—and it became a four-way shootout, bullets swarming like so many hornets, furious at violation of their nest.

Bursting through the back door of the house on Bristol Avenue, Stan Dartnell found himself inside a well-appointed kitchen, blacked out, but the lights from an adjacent room reflected from a rack of hanging copper pots and pans along one side. Ahead of him, he heard two angry voices quarreling, then shooting started and his destination toward the street side turned into a free-fire zone.

Pistols, which didn't worry him too much, although a stray round or a ricochet could still prove fatal, even if the shooters didn't realize that they had company. Men cursing, some of it in Russian, which he did not speak but recognized by sound. Mostly nine-millimeter gunfire, although one weapon in the three-way fight was lighter, possible a .32 or .380.

Discerning weapons by their sound could be a life-saver,

even for soldiers trained as designated marksmen trained specifically for killing at long range.

Dartnell moved toward the battle sounds, along a short hallway, to reach a living room. Or maybe he should make that "dying" room, the way its occupants were pumping rounds at one another. Reg knew none of them by sight but guessed the two facing in his direction were the late arrivals Grant Mahoney had reported closing in on the snuff film director's house from Bristol Avenue.

That made the third guy, with his back toward Stan, Aaron Yablonsky, verified by airport carryon-sized luggage lying on the carpet at his feet.

It happened fast once Dartnell reached the once-domestic killing ground. He didn't bother shouting for the gunmen to discard their arms, knowing they wouldn't have obeyed even if they could hear and understand him. Sent to pluck Aaron Yablonsky from the house, Stan focused on the target's adversaries first, never forgetting that the man his team had come to snatch and grill for information still might turn and kill him, given half a chance.

Stan had his M4 carbine set for three-round bursts, spotting the nearer of the Russian speakers first, the guy on his right, planting the Aimpoint sight's red dot dead-center on a heaving body-builder's chest inside a T-shirt blazoned with the logo of some band whose name meant nothing to him. Stan's 5.56mm rounds propelled the shooter, dying, backwards toward a window that someone had broken from the inside, probably to fire at Dartnell's four companions on the street.

That left two gunmen standing, with the second Russian bleeding from a belly wound. Surprisingly, instead of trying to drop Dartnell with his automatic, he pumped close-range bullets toward Yablonsky, hitting home with two or three of them before Stan could adjust his sights and send another burst to finish it.

A little higher up that time, and Dartnell saw the scowling Russian's face implode, spraying the nearest wall with gray and crimson muck as he went down. Between the falling hitman and Dartnell, Yablonsky—who else could it be?—collapsed onto the floor, allowing Stan to close the gap between them and disarm him finally.

"All clear!" he shouted to his friends outside, and in another moment they were with him, standing in a semicircle, peering at the man they'd come in search of.

"He's still breathing," Natalie Karpin observed.

Grant Mahoney knelt beside Yablonsky, checking first to make sure that he missed the blood already soaking into carpet fibers there. He used one hand to elevate the snuff director's head without straining his neck too much.

"You're done," Grant told their target. "Black blood means one of the slugs is in your liver. Cope are on the way, but even if we phoned right now it's too late for an ambulance."

Yablonsky grimaced, coughed and blew a bubble that burst on his lips, streaking his chin and cheeks bright red. "Who…who are you?" he demanded.

"Not important now," Mahoney answered him. "You still have time to do one decent thing. We're after Carrie Maddox. If you tell us where to find her—"

The director made a wheezing sound and spat more blood onto himself. It might have been ironic laughter or a death rattle. Dartnell could not have told the two apart.

"Don't know," Yablonsky gasped. "Have to…ask Joel."

"Who's Joel?" Grant asked him, giving the near-corpse a little shake when it appeared Yablonsky might be fading out. And once again, "Who's Joel?"

"Carmichael," Aaron burbled. "Producer. Money man. He set it up with…"

The words trailed off and stopped. Yablonsky's head sagged back against Mahoney's firm supporting hand and he was history.

Grant cursed, released his grip on the director's neck and let his head drop backward to the floor. He rose, glanced toward the street, where Stan and all the rest of them heard sirens closing from a half-mile out or less.

"Joel Carmichael," Mahoney said. "Must be a few of those scattered around New York."

"I'll try to pare it down," his brother said. "But now—"

"We need to go," Grant finished for him. Told the others, "Back to the hotel for now."

Dartnell turned and retraced his steps to exit through the kitchen, out the back, across the dead man's lawn to reach his car parked in the alley. Rolling out, he wondered whether Blake could trace the name their target had provided, or if it would prove to be one last dead end.

10

Midtown Manhattan

As it turned out, Blake searching on his laptop back at their East 33rd Street lodgings, there were only two Joel Carmichaels on record in the city's five boroughs. One was a senior citizen, unmarried, living in Gowanus, Brooklyn. Number two, a freshman at Harvey Milk High School, resided with his parents and a younger brother in Manhattan's East Village.

Obviously, neither one of them held any interest for the SFX team's manhunters.

Expanding his search beyond Gotham, Blake finally hit on a third prospect, living in Jersey City, opposite Lower Manhattan on the west side of the Hudson River. And that time, Mahoney knew he'd hit the jackpot.

Joel Carmichael III possessed what cops or journalists might call "a history." All people did, of course, but Carmichael's was different, evocative. He came from old money, last of the line as far as Blake could tell, and her had squandered most of it on high living before it struck him that he ought to be a film producer. Short of useful contacts in show business, Carmichael went the independent route, investing what remained of his family fortune and seeing fair returns from it with cut-rate softcore exploitation films employing various unknowns, until stiff competition from the major studios out west dried up his profit margin.

Next, he'd set his sights on porn, both gay and "straight," willing to grind out anything that might return a dollar, mixing seasoned pros who mostly phoned it in with more enthusiastic amateurs, a few of whom went on to bigger, slightly better things in time. Again, Carmichael's hopes were swept away, this time in a tsunami of direct-to-video productions shot on shoestring budgets, catering to fans who liked their hardcore hard and mostly eyeballed it at home, instead of patronizing low-rent Times Square theaters.

Blake couldn't prove it from his online search, but it appeared that Carmichael had reached the nadir of his "craft" with snuff, although the FBI's archives and NYPD's files had nothing that would tie him to a felony, much less serial murder as a business venture. What they *did* have was a string of leaks from various CI's—confidential informants who earned pocket money squealing to the law—that linked Carmichael to the Gotham underworld.

His friendships, when it came to gangland, were eclectic and discreet, though not invisible. One of his known associates was Mafioso Angelo Rizzo. Another, also linked to Rizzo through a string of shady ventures, was a Russian immigrant, ex-con and *bratva* captain based in Brighton Beach, Shamil Povetkin.

Not exactly paydirt, granted, but at least it was a start.

When Blake had laid it out for Grant and their comrades, the vote turned out to be unanimous. Joel Carmichael III was worth a closer look, some pointed questions, whatever it took to find out how and why he was connected to Aaron Yablonsky, snuff director.

"The feds have nothing on him?" Grant inquired, when Blake had finished with his briefing.

"No surprise," Blake said, "since they claim snuff films

are an urban myth. And jurisdiction-wise, NYPD can't lay a finger on him in New Jersey."

There had been a time when Gotham mobsters pulled up stakes and moved to Jersey, ducking heat in the five boroughs, and the Garden State harbored its own established mobs. As far as snuff films went, NYPD seemed satisfied to take the FBI's word that a fairy tale could do no harm to anyone. That freed them up to keep a closer eye on Muslims, labor agitators, and Antifa activists who liked to give riotous neo-Nazis a harsh taste of their own medicine.

"So, Jersey City," Natalie observed.

"A suburb of it on the Hudson, Paulus Hook," Blake clarified. "We'd take the Holland Tunnel over to Newport, then head south on Marin Boulevard and east on Grand Street. Carmichael's on Washington, a long block south of Grand."

"No way of knowing if he's home? Maybe a pretext call?" asked Hardy.

"Wouldn't want to tip him off and make him bolt," Grant said.

The former SAS man nodded. "I hear that. When do we roll?"

"Right now," told his team.

Each carrying a duffel bag containing his or her M4 and various spare magazines, they left Mahoney's suite and headed for the elevator that would take them down to the below-ground parking lot. Three rented cars, with the Mahoney brothers teamed, Hardy and Dartnell doubled up, and Natalie riding alone.

Among them all, only Dartnell, oddly, had ever passed through Jersey City, and his visit there had not included Paulus Hook. They had reviewed the maps on Google Earth and had the route for their procession memorized, however, with the estimates of driving time based on traffic. The Holland Tunnel was a bottleneck, but they would make it.

Now they only had to worry about Joel Carmichael staying put at home until they dropped in unannounced.

Paulus Hook, New Jersey

Initially the site of a Revolutionary War fortress and a battle waged in 1779, Paulus Hook was later developed by Dutch settlers, named for a prominent founder plus *hoeck,* translated into English as "point of land." Establishment of railroad links, ferry service and light industry encouraged expansion, deterred briefly by flooding from Hurricane Sandy in October 2012.

Joel Carmichael III enjoyed New Jersey living as a get-away from Gotham, including the Garden State's dramatically lower tax rates—not that he'd ever paid his full debt to a given jurisdiction in his life. From the beginning, he'd been schooled by family accountants in the fine art of evading taxes, and when that fortune ran out, new tricks unique to show business ensured that Carmichael's deductions constantly exceeded revenue.

And that was just the income that the feds and treasury in Trenton knew about. As far as what he'd stashed away in the Bahamas, in the Caymans and Belize…well, what the auditors were unaware of couldn't hurt him.

If the axe fell on his latest enterprise—a possibility that he could not ignore—Carmichael reckoned it would be the FBI that came to snatch him, maybe helped along by Customs, with the IRS running a distant third.

His portion of the Maddox ransom, plus whatever extra pay-off he could add to that by playing angles known but to himself and one other conspirator, would set him up for life. It might not be enough to set him up for life, retiring at a relatively youthful forty years of age, but with persuasive fake I.D., maybe a bogus death certificate to make it stick, he could start over somewhere else and build another splendid fortune for himself.

Example: one of the most violent, notorious Klan leaders in America during the 1980s—forced to drop that cash cow when he was exposed as an informer for the FBI—had popped up later in Belize, proud owner of a luxury resort for fat-cat tourists of all creeds and colors in San Pedro, ritzy condos overlooking the Caribbean, where everyone in town knew him under his birth name and ignored his rancid record from those bygone days.

Imagine what a man of Carmichael's imagination and experience could manage once he had remade himself entirely, with nothing to link him with his past.

And if he kept his hand in with the outlaw movie trade, discreetly, at arm's length, there was no reason that he should not wallow in the proceeds for another twenty, even thirty years.

At this moment, though, the smart thing was to bail out and lie low.

Ready to roll now, checking in with his associate Shamil Povetkin at the Russian's urging, Carmichael turned to Clete Rothman, chief of the security detachment he'd assembled to patrol his small estate in Paulus Hook—the house snide social critics liked to call "McMansions" these days—with four acres of immaculately tended property surrounding it.

Clete was a lucky find: a former Special Forces Green Beret who'd served time in "the sand" and then retired with no illusions of "my country right or wrong." The small force of a dozen other vets that he commanded, broken into three-man shifts, had skills on par with Rothman's and took orders as if they still drew their pay from Uncle Sam, but with a better health plan if they suffered job-related injury.

Carmichael did not bother asking whether Clete knew where to reach him in the case of an emergency. He'd left Povetkin's private number, just in case, but wasn't counting on an interruption now, when they were only hours out from picking up the Maddox ransom and deciding what would happen next.

Of course, they'd promised safe return of Carrie Maddox, but that wasn't happening. Had never been intended from the start. Even when dosed with ketamine she'd seen too many faces, might have sobered up and figured out too much to risk her spilling what she knew or *thought* she knew to Daddy, ranked by friends and foes alike as one of the country's most powerful senators—number four or five, some said, after the aging Majority Leader himself.

Worse yet, a legislator who could twist innumerable arms in law enforcement, bend Attorneys General and FBI Directors to his will with threats of Senate inquisitions or an interrupted flow of federal appropriations to their agencies.

Daddy would be enraged after he'd paid the ransom and got nothing in return except an empty chair beside his dining table during holidays in Richmond, but when Darling Daughter simply disappeared, what could the old man do about it?

Flog his underlings to find the smallest clue, of course, but if there were no clues, even a fierce, relentless bloodhound must exhaust himself in time. And he was no spring chicken, only had a few years left for "public service," whittled down by private loss and heartbreak, with some nagging health issues the finest doctors couldn't cure.

All Joel Carmichael had to do was wait the old man out, be cool until he croaked and Carrie's disappearance passed into the realm of greatest unsolved modern mysteries.

"Okay, I'm going," he told Rothman. "Only call if it's a *serious* emergency."

"Yes, sir."

It was a short walk from the front door to Carmichael's waiting Mercedes-Benz E-Class sedan, equipped with "Car-to-X" technology that offered advance in-car updates of approaching road hazards, a PRE-SAFE sound system that sensed impending collisions, emitting "pink noise" to shield delicate eardrums during collisions, and an Impulse Side feature that rapidly inflated front-seat bolsters to insulate the driver from impacts.

Tonight, riding alone, Carmichael only had to travel eighteen miles—say forty minutes if the lights were mostly green—and then he could relax until the ransom money was delivered.

After that, he'd be as good as gold.

The night was winding down and Grant Mahoney felt time slipping through his fingers. They'd made progress rattling cages, and he hoped for more in Paulus Hook, but he could not escape a sense that Carrie Maddox must be running out of hope.

And whether the SFX team could rescue her remained an open question.

"Not too shabby for a guy that couldn't make a go with skin-flicks," Blake observed, eyeing their latest target's house and grounds.

"I still wish we knew more about him," Grant replied. "It doesn't track for me why someone in the skin trade, even at the dark end, should step out of character and try a ransom snatch."

"It isn't that far-fetched," Blake said. "If he's been living off the dregs of human trafficking this far, why not try for a bigger payday?"

"I can't put my finger on it yet," Grant answered, "but it doesn't feel like something he'd come up with on his own."

"You could be right, bro. Let's find out, shall we?"

A call-around by walkie-talkie found the other members of their team on station, ready to proceed. Grant gave the order, started toward the big house with his brother, thankful that their man had not constructed looming walls around his acreage to rile the neighbors.

Still, they were alert for lookouts on patrol and found one within moments, standing in the shadow of a stately sculpted oak, trying to will himself invisible. Grant gave him points for effort but a glint of moonlight from the barrel of a submachine gun he was carrying betrayed his effort.

There were two ways they could take him down: lethal or

nonlethal. Blake did the honors, coming up behind the gun-man with a sap and striking him behind one ear, catching the body as it slumped into unconsciousness. Twist ties secured the watchman's wrists and ankles, while a gag forestalled him crying out for help.

Grant hoped that they would not regret sparing his life.

He clicked the walkie-talkie twice to tell his comrades that one threat had been eliminated. Moments later, double clicks resounded from the night, meaning that two more lookouts had been neutralized.

Blake held the two-way radio he had collected from the man he'd blackjacked, had it turned on with the volume low. When they were near the house, a man's voice came over the air, announcing, "Time check. Number One?"

No answer came. A second fruitless call to Number One was followed swiftly by demands for prompt acknowledgement from Number Two and Number Three, each time without result.

"Sounds like they're short of guards," Blake said.

"That could be Carmichael," Grant offered.

"Or he's got a houseman managing the others."

Either way, at least one occupant was on alert to danger now, and likely armed. Grant made it fifty-fifty as to whether he—or they—would call for aid from the police. Less likely if Carmichael was, in fact, involved in kidnapping and snuff films. No one in that position would invite official scrutiny except in desperation, as a last resort.

They closed in on the house, Grant picturing Dartnell, Hardy and Karpin steadily advancing through darkness. As they approached the structure from its front side, facing toward Washington Street. From a hundred feet out, they saw a man emerge onto the porch, holding an H&K MP5 submachine gun, left hand raised to press an earpiece as he called again for recognition from his guards.

"That isn't Carmichael," Blake said.

Grant had been with him when they studied dated photos of their target, snapped years earlier at an AVN Awards ceremony—*Adult Video News*, that was—when he'd been nominated as Best Director for his feature *Private Party.* Someone else had edged Carmichael out and snagged the trophy that portrayed a naked couple snogging, but the nominees had all been photographed and featured in the trades.

"Looks like he knows his way around that MP5," said.

"Disabling shot?" Grant asked his brother.

"That would be my preference."

"Flip for it?"

Blake already had the M4 carbine at his shoulder, smiling to himself.

"Relax, bro," he told Grant. "Watch how it's done."

Clete Rothman never knew what hit him. By the time a muzzle flash had registered, before the echo of a single gunshot reached his ears, he was already lying on his back, sprawled on Carmichael's porch, the pain in his right shoulder ramping up from dull impact to pulsing agony.

Clete didn't scream, had learned to sublimate his pain, hold it together, even when he realized that he'd effectively been taken out of action. Trying to retrieve his MP5, he managed no reaction from his right arm, and trying to roll in that direction, groping with his left, the misery of pressure on his mangled shoulder nearly blacked him out.

He thought next of his pistol, slung under his left arm in a Jackass shoulder rig, and was attempting to dislodge it when a man's voice cautioned him, "I wouldn't."

Five strangers surrounded him, four men and one woman who looked as tough as any of the rest, all aiming M4 carbines at Clete's supine form.

"My men?" he asked through gritted teeth.

"Alive and well," one of the men standing above him said.

"You can swap stories with them if you make it through the night."

"And what's that gonna take?" Rothman enquired.

"We're looking for your boss.

Rothman considered that. When he was serving with the U.S. Army Special Forces there had been a certain protocol. If captured, you gave up your name, rank and serial number, no more and no less. Beyond that, he'd been schooled in withstanding interrogation, drilled in escape and evasion procedures, but Clete had left all that behind when he was discharged to civilian life, hawking his martial skills to the highest bidder.

Silence was no longer a matter or honor and duty to service or homeland.

Bottom line: it was a sure-fire way to get him killed.

"I'm bleeding out here," Clete advised his captors.

"You've still got some time," one the grim-faced men replied. "We need to talk before you see a medic."

"Sure. Okay," said Rothman. "What's the subject."

"Take a guess," the only female in the circle said.

"My boss, right?"

"Twenty questions squeezed down into two, mate," said a guy who sounded British. "Where'd he go and who's his boss?"

"One answer covers both," Clete said.

"No hesitation?" said another of the men, frowning.

"He pays me to protect him, then takes off and dumps the heat on me. I'd call that breach of contract."

"So," one of the men, an Aussie accent this time asked," is there an answer in our future?"

"Carmichael had two men over him that I'm aware of. One's a goombah name of Angelo Rizzo. The other one's a Russian *vor y zakone*. That means—"

"A thief-in-law," the woman finished for him. "From the *russkaya mafiya*."

"Right. Okay. This *vor* is named Shamil Povetkin. Lives in Brighton Beach, where most of them hang out. I never got the address, but he shouldn't be that hard to find if you've got resources."

"And you say Carmichael is on his way to meet Povetkin now?" one of the two gunmen who looked a bit alike inquired.

"Unless he lied to me before he left. That's always possible I guess," Chet said. "I'd call his cell no matter where he is. The number's saved up on my phone. Left trouser pocket."

The woman fished it out. Rothman resisted his first impulse to crack wise.

"Got it," she told her friends."

"There's one more thing you ought to know," Chet said. They have a fourth hand in this bridge game they've got going on. Can't help you with a name and never caught a glimpse, but when they talk amongst themselves they always mention 'she'."

"A woman?" said the babe who'd copped his phone.

"Or else a trannie," Rothman answered. "But I doubt they're that evolved, know that I mean? Doubtful they ever heard of something called 'politically correct'."

"Okay, then," said the seeming leader of the firing squad. "You have a good night, hear?"

"Hey, wait a second! If you're leaving with my phone…"

"A place this size," the woman said, "there must be half a dozen scattered through the house, at least."

"Just crawl around in there—"

"And if you get the urge to somebody with a badge what happened here, maybe describe us to a sketch artist, I suspect that your prognosis could nose-dive from 'guarded' straight to 'terminal'."

"I hear you, man."

"I hope so," said their mouthpiece, then they turned away and melted back into the Jersey City night.

11

Brightwater Drive, Brighton Beach

Shamil Povetkin lived three blocks from Café Moskva, in a building that had once housed six apartments. He had purchased it, relocated the aged tenants, and then renovated it from top to bottom, making it a home that any *vor* might envy.

Joel Carmichael found it garish, as if nightclub decorators high on meth had run amok, trying to recreate a nightmare version of Hugh Hefner's Playboy Mansion from the Sixties, but never would have said that to the Russian's face. Would not have dared unless he craved a beating or a razor-slashing. Better just to smile and say, "How cool is that?"

Tonight the snuff producer did not feel like putting on an act. His summons meant that something had gone wrong, their master plan was starting to unravel, though Povetkin would not brief him on the telephone. Strict orders to arrive without delay, present himself before The Man—or one of them, at least.

He wondered whether Angelo The Animal would also be attending, braced himself for anything as a valet relieved him of the key to his Mercedes-Benz, another of Povetkin's goons escorted him inside the Russian's monument to an inflated vision of himself. He trailed his escort past the life-sized sculptures of nude women writhing in contorted poses to a library where he had spoken with Povetkin twice before. The very presence of a well-stocked library struck Joel as ironic, since he harbored a suspicion that Povetkin was illiterate.

A possibility that no one in his right mind would confuse with being stupid.

"Ah, my friend!" Povetkin greeted him, as if surprised to see Carmichael suddenly appear.

Carmichael glanced around the library, no sign of Rizzo anywhere, and let himself relax a bit. Not much, but just enough to stop himself from trembling visibly.

"You said there was a problem?" he inquired.

"And straight to business. I admire that," Shamil said. "But first, perhaps a taste of vodka? I have Beluga Gold Line Noble, Grey Goose, Crystal Head?"

"No, thank you. I'm just here—"

"Because I hope to save your life," Povetkin interrupted him.

"Excuse me?"

"*Da*. We've come under attack. The senator, it seems, desires to challenge us and disregard his daughter's safety."

"What? Attack?"

"A series of attacks, in fact. I don't have all the details yet, but I can say that Courtney Bennett has gone missing, with Diego Báez and Aaron Yablonsky."

Joel gaped at his host. "All three of them? Tonight?"

"And Brady Connors," said Povetkin. "I forgot about him."

"Who?" Carmichael didn't recognize the name.

"I don't believe you've met him," Shamil said, "and now it seems you've missed your chance. He helped facilitate the Maddox girl's abduction."

"Jesus Christ!"

"I seriously doubt He was involved."

"You drop this in my lap and think it's *funny*?"

"On the contrary, *moy drug*. I take it very seriously."

"How can this be happening? Why didn't she—"

"Alert us?" Shamil finished Joel's thought for him. "We *were* advised that Maddox was recruiting help outside the normal law enforcement channels, but it sounded as if he was hiring 'private eyes,' I think you call them in *Amerika*."

"But you were wrong," Carmichael said, his stomach slowly knotting.

"That would seem to be the case, alas. Instead of television's Magnum, we have mercenaries now, apparently collaborating with the government."

Carmichael felt his gourmet dinner threatening to make a reappearance on Povetkin's carpet, fought down that sensation. Said, "All right. I'm getting out of here."

"That won't be possible," Povetkin cautioned him.

"Ex*cuse* me?"

"You and I are, how you say it, in this thing together? Also our good friend *zhivotnoye*."

"Say what?"

"The Animal, as people call him."

Carmichael felt dizzy, couldn't seem to grasp the import of Povetkin's words.

"Rizzo is coming here?" he asked.

"*Nyet.* We are going now to meet him at a safer place.

"What? Where?" But then it hit Joel, and the answer, still unspoken by Povetkin, frightened him. "Why there? We should be bailing out before these mercenaries or whatever track us down. Gathering together in one place is—"

"What?" Povetkin challenged him.

Carmichael had been on the verge of calling Shamil's idea stupid, idiotic, possibly insane, but now he caught himself. "Too risky?"

Making it a question sounded safer.

"On the contrary, *moy drug*. Safety in numbers is my motto, as you say. Now, if you're ready, we should go."

"This doesn't look like much," said Blake Mahoney.

Brother Grant replied, "Don't let it fool you. Our guy has the whole place to himself with room to spare. No telling how he's fortified the place since he took over.

The building's bland façade was painted gray, drapes drawn across its windows on all three floors, nothing that would make it stand out from its neighboring structures on Brightwater Drive. From floorplans accessed on the Web, Blake knew its renovation on the inside had been radical, combining various former apartments into one three-story space. The ground floor housed a living room, library, dining room and kitchen, bathroom, and a rec room at the rear. The second floor included five bedrooms for bodyguards or guests, each with an en suite bathroom. The whole top floor was one spacious apartment featuring a boudoir, entertainment center, and a bathroom larger than the second-story bedrooms, featuring a bath, shower and hot tub.

Everything a rising *vor y zakone* could wish for in a starter home.

"A lot of room for shooters," Blake advised.

"Won't know who's home until we get inside," Grant said.

Back at their San Diego headquarters, the SFX team had a stash of gear including Range-R motion-sensing radar, Eye-max Spy Snake fiber optic cameras and other high-tech tools that let them see through solid walls, but they'd shipped none of it back east when summoned to the conference at Foley Square. Tonight, they would be crashing hostile territory with a builder's blueprint fixed in mind and nothing else.

And what could possibly go wrong?

Against uncertain odds, a bit of anything and everything.

Their weapons double-checked and good to go, the warriors fanned out to surround Shamil Povetkin's home and likely headquarters. The brothers took the front approach,

Brightwater Avenue, facing the Riegelman Boardwalk. Reg Hardy closed in from the west, Stan Dartnell from the east. Natalie Karpin took the rear approach, walking across dead ground from Seacoast Terrace.

They went in with watches synchronized, prepared to strike on the half hour, booting doors and dropping anyone who tried to block them from their primary targets. Joel Carmichael was number one,. The Russian mobster who collaborated with and possibly controlled him ran a close second and might turn out to be a more important mark than Carmichael himself.

Two men they hoped—*needed*—to take alive.

As for the rest, hired guns had always been disposable.

And so were they, when Grant Mahoney thought about it, working for a U.S. senator whose only real concern was being reunited safely with his daughter. Any thought that Harlan Maddox cared about the pawns he'd hired to do his bidding was a fantasy.

There hadn't been much time to scout security before they struck, spotting strategic CCTV cameras positioned at each corner of Povetkin's home, no way of knowing whether monitors inside were manned around the clock or only watched haphazardly by lazy guards. Whatever, if they went in fast and hard enough, Grant thought they had a fighting chance.

Beyond that estimation, everything was up for grabs.

He fired a three-round carbine burst into the front door's locks and kicked it open, charging through with brother Blake close on his heels.

"Christ, that was close!"

Joel Carmichael was startled by the raspy tenor of his own voice as Shamil Povetkin's Curti Zefhir two-seat helicopter lifted off and spiraled skyward, rising swiftly from its helipad atop his home on Brightwater. Its twin rotors were powered by a PBS Velká Bíteš TS100 turboshaft motor, boosting the ultralight chopper's 1,540 pounds toward its top speed of 115 miles per hour, with a service ceiling of 13,000 feet.

As down below, a raiding team was smashing into Shamil's home.

"How did you know?" Carmichael asked Povetkin, who seemed cool as ice at the Zefhir's controls.

"I was not certain," his airborne chauffeur replied, "but I have learned to play the odds."

Carmichael didn't know where they were going, but Shamil had told him that the Zefhir's range was just a tick under two hundred miles. From Brighton Beach they could touch down at JFK or Newark Liberty International, Atlantic City, Trenton, Teterboro, or a couple dozen other airports scattered over New York and New Jersey, before starting to consider private landing fields of which Carmichael had no knowledge.

Getting out of Brighton Beach wasn't the problem.

That arose when he considered touching down again.

"Who were those people?" he inquired, addressing Shamil through the throat mic that connected to his padded earphones, cutting back the helicopter's scream to a dull roar.

Povetkin shrugged. "Who knows? The people Maddox hired to find his little girl, presumably."

Well, shit! Carmichael's mind was racing, weighing odds against survival first, and then escape. When they'd begun this madness, he'd been fool enough to think it sounded easy, what Angelo Rizzo called "a snap," but now the thing had blown up in their faces and Carmichael wondered when his life would start to flash before his eyes in preparation for the bitter end.

Strangers with guns were hunting him, were hunting all of them, and from Povetkin's rundown of the situation they were not police, not FBI, not bound by any rules of conduct under law.

Unable to accept responsibility for that himself, Carmichael knew exactly who to blame —not that it mattered in the least or helped even a little now.

Even if he could reach out through the night and take revenge, who could he really blame for his present predicament?

The snuff film racket was not Carmichael's idea, but when presented with the opportunity, the chance to make a fortune with what seemed to be a minimum of risk, he'd had no second thoughts. No scruples about profiting from murder and the twisted appetites of freaks he deemed inferior in all respects, even while catering to their sadistic whims.

He'd gone along to get along, and now Carmichael recognized that he might well be running out of time.

"So, what's the plan?" he asked Povetkin. Was prepared to ask again as precious seconds ticked away, before the Russian finally acknowledged hearing him.

"First stop," Shamil said at last, "there is a hideaway I have prepared. Rizzo will meet us there. I will send men to fetch the girl and those in charge of her. You are prepared to leave the country, I assume?"

"I am," Carmichael said, although he'd never planned that it would be so soon.

"No problem, then," Shamil assured him. "We collect the ransom, clean house, and depart."

Carmichael blinked, wondering if Povetkin had already lost his mind. Collect the ransom? Seriously?

Blanking out the madness of that notion, Carmichael dismissed the Russian from his thoughts and focused on the primary imperative.

From now on, he was strictly looking out for Number One.

But if he saw an opportunity for settling accounts, exacting vengeance…well he'd be a fool to pass it up.

And if he couldn't do that right away, so what? Once he'd escaped to any one of eighty-three nations lacking any extradition treaties with the States, there would be ample time to plot and scheme.

As somebody or other, name long lost to history, once rightly said, revenge was a dish best served cold.

Floorplans aside, the SFX team knew within seconds of entering Shamil Povetkin's home that he had more than five soldiers on hand.

At least that many opened up on Grant and Blake Mahoney as they crashed the first floor with their M4 carbines poised to answer hostile fire with three-round 5.56mm bursts. The shooters weren't exposed, lined up like members of a firing squad, but muzzle flashes from their weapons winked from open doorways and behind expensive furniture.

The brothers broke for cover, hunkered down, and started potting targets that were barely visible. With NATO rounds flying more than half a mile per second, sofas, La-Z-Boys and plaster walls provided less protection than the home team may have hoped. One guy spilled from a doorway, twitching, and another gasped a dying cry of pain behind a sofa that had likely cost at least three grand, his submachine gun dropping into view from spastic fingers.

About that time, Grant heard more shooting from the rear end of the house, where he supposed Natalie must have entered right on time. No sooner had those echoes started rolling through the house, than firing started from his left and right, the other SFX team members bursting in, still out of sight.

A tall man with a sawed-off shotgun fired a buckshot blast toward Blake's point of concealment but misjudged the range and took the head off a rendition of the classical Venus de Milo, this one wholly nude, with its right arm replaced, hand thrust between splayed legs. Decapitated, it fell forward, stuck the floor, and broke into a dozen pieces on impact.

Blake dropped that shooter with his next short burst, stitched not-so-tidy holes across his chest and bounced him off a nearby door frame, toppling forward, landing facedown with the shotgun pinned beneath him.

There were only two defenders still in action, caught inside a closing ring of steel. The SFX commandos had no time for conversation as they dealt with those, confirming afterward that none of those they'd slain matched mug shots of Shamil Povetkin or the photographs of Joel Carmichael found online.

"We missed them, people," Natalie advised, as they perused the corpses.

"Thought I heard a chopper, faintly," Grant allowed. "Hoped I was wrong."

"You weren't," Nat said. "It took off just as I was coming in. An ultralight, one of those two-seaters. I couldn't see the tail numbers."

Dartnell and Hardy took turns cursing rotten luck. Blake said, "It didn't show up on the Google Earth photos."

"Povetkin likely stows it somewhere else until he needs it," Grant suggested.

"So, you think he knew that we were coming, bro?" Blake asked.

"Maybe. Or else he got wind of the other people he's been losing. Thought he'd take it on the lam."

A shifting sound upstairs distracted them.

"Somebody else is still at home," said Hardy.

Grant Mahoney checked his watch and estimated timing of the first police response. "Let's go on up," he said. "See who it is."

Had anyone been rash enough to question Uri Levanevski on the subject, he would have he would readily have told them that he was a brave man, battle-tested, blooded on the mean streets of Saint Petersburg and then in prison, finally in the United States, where he had risen to the rank of houseman under Shamil Povetkin. His cars and various tattoos were testimony to that fact.

Tonight, though left behind to hold an indefensible position against unknown enemies, Uri was not so sure.

Gunfire had ended on the ground floor of Povetkin's garish mansion now, and Levanevski had not ventured down the stairs to help him men. Of eight *soldaty* detailed to protect the house when Shamil literally flew the coop with his *amerikanskiy* visitor, no room for any others in their little helicopter, only Uri and Gennady Brusilov remained. By now, Uri assumed, the others must be dead.

Good men, at least for what they were, but clearly they had not been good enough.

Gennady was the first to hear footsteps coming upstairs. He hissed and nodded to alert the man Shamil had left in charge, clutching his AK-101 assault rifle against his chest, hands clenched as if to stop them trembling, knuckles blanched.

"Be ready," Levanevski ordered in a harsh whisper. "Cover the stairs."

Brusilov blinked at him, then bobbed his head and went to do as he'd been ordered, even knowing that it likely meant his death. Uri admired that, wish he could have done as well, but something on the inside of him—nerve, or what Americans called "heart"—was wavering about to effervesce and seep out through his pores like sweat.

Uri retreated to the nearest bedroom door and opened it, concealed himself behind its jamb, gripping his stubby MP5K submachine gun tight enough to make his hands ache. The weapon weighed two kilograms—less than five pounds—and measured only 14.5 inches with its stock folded but fired nine hundred rounds per minute to the parent MP5's eight hundred rpm.

Alas, that meant its thirty-round box magazine would be exhausted in two seconds flat of fully automatic fire.

And Uri Levanevski only had one extra magazine to spare.

So he could fight for just four seconds, then fall back upon his sidearm, a Beretta 92, loaded—like his little SMG—with

9×19mm Parabellum rounds, two spare mags slotted into leather pouches on his belt. In theory, that would buy Uri another minute, more or less, and then he'd be effectively unarmed.

Which meant he would be dead.

So be it. From the time he'd joined the *bratva* as a young man in the Gulag, such had always been his destiny.

Few who adopted a *kriminal'naya zhizn'*—a life of crime—lived to enjoy their so-called golden years.

Gennady started shouting curses down the staircase leading to the ground floor, firing short bursts from his AK-101, inviting swift retaliation from below. From where he stood, half-hidden, Levanevski saw the last surviving member of his house team taking hits, lurching and reeling backwards to collapse upon the second-story landing, heels drumming on carpet in his death throes.

Now it was Uri's turn.

He saw the first of stranger, an enemy, step into view on the second-floor landing. Levaneski was about to hose the landing with his MP5K but a jerky movement of his hand betrayed him. Even as he squeezed the SMG's trigger, his intended target ducked low, hit the floor, and fired off half a dozen 5.56mm rounds. The nearest of them struck the doorjamb half an inch from Uri's face and blinded him with jagged wooden splinters, causing him to flinch and miss his mark.

More guns were spitting at him then, one slug drilling his thigh, snapping the femur like a twig. Another struck his SMG and splintered, driving copper fragments into Levanevski's biceps and armpit. He staggered, crying out in pain, and dropped the MP5K as he stumbled, reeled and fell.

In seconds flat he was surrounded, five shapes looming over him, one kicking his machine pistol away and out of reach. Five rifles angles toward his face and chest, prepared to riddle him if he made one false move.

"Do not shoot more!" he begged, humiliated. "I need

medical attention!"

"Tell someone who cares," one of the gunmen sneered at him. For the first time, discovered one of his assailants was female. Speaking to her, hoping that she could still feel pity, he inquired, "What do you want here?"

She said nothing, but the man who'd spoken earlier replied, "We're looking for your boss."

"And for his guest," another said. "Joel Carmichael."

"They've gone," said Levanevski, speaking truthfully.

"Gone where?" the woman said at last, her voice ice-cold.

"They did not say, just took—"

"The helicopter," she said, talking over him. "I saw it leave. It has to land somewhere."

"My boss goes anywhere he likes. I only have his phone number."

Uri was reaching toward a pocket for his cell phone, when the M4 carbines moved a trifle closer—or was a trick of his imagination.

"Careful there," The woman cautioned him. "Two fingers. Make it slow."

Uri produced his phone and flipped it toward her feet. The four men covered him while she bend to retrieve it, turned it on, then asked him, "Does the helicopter have a GPS tracker installed."

"Yes!" Levanevski felt an idiot, guessing he should have mentioned that himself. "Dial 5-1-1 to activate the app."

The woman followed his direction, then handed the phone to one of her companions. He peered at the screen, told his associates, "Heading northwest from here." Turning to Uri once again, he asked, "What's up that way?"

"I don't...Oh, wait! Most likely they will go to Clifton. That is forty miles or so away. Povetkin has property there, larger than here in Brighton Beach. There is an airstrip that he uses and a large house walled around."

"What does he do in Clifton?" asked the man still holding Levanevski's phone."

"Relaxes I suppose," Uri replied. "And sometimes they make films. You know? Movies?"

"Movies. You don't mind if I take your phone along?" the man inquired.

"No, no. Please do. If you could only call an ambulance before you leave?"

"About that," said the woman, sighting down the barrel of her carbine at his face. "You won't be needing one."

12

Clifton, New Jersey

Shamil Povetkin's home away from home was located on Grove Street in far southwest Clifton, sandwiched between Immaculate Conception Cemetery and Alonzo F. Bonsai Wildlife Preserve. Well separate from its nearest neighbors, it had privacy, seclusion, and was owned on paper by a corporation chartered in the name of two dead men.

What happened there, for the most part, remained a secret of Povetkin, his invited guests, and those he paid to keep their mouths shut under threat of execution.

Some of his snuff films had been produced there in a soundproofed bungalow. The "actors" who did not survive were variously weighted down in Boonton Reservoir, some in the Hudson River, or buried in the New Jersey Pine Barrens, sprawling over seven counties—1.1 million square miles—that constituted 22 percent of the Garden State's total area.

So far, none had been dredged up or unearthed.

Joel Carmichael III, alighting from Povetkin's Curti Zefhir helicopter in the spacious backyard of a rambling house, knew all that information but was not concerned about it now. His mind was focused on surviving through the night, and where he might wind up tomorrow.

Was a safe haven awaiting him, or would his final destination be a woodland grave, a lake's bottom, or a polluted river that disgorged him into the Atlantic? Was there any justice in the world today for such as he?

Carmichael hoped not, kept his fingers crossed, but did not prove himself a hypocrite by praying to some god long cast aside.

Povetkin's second home was old, constructed out of brick and stone, with heavy beams supporting gabled roofs built to withstand New Jersey's winter snow. The grounds, extensive, were surrounded by high walls, encompassing a swimming pool its owner loved and tennis courts that he would never use, although some of his guests—the ones at liberty to come and go—enjoyed in spring and summer.

From the great house, visitors could barely glimpse the combination bungalow and studio where films and videos were shot and victims screamed their vocal cords to bloody shreds during production of a feature running thirty minutes on the average.

As huckster P. T. Barnum once proclaimed, a showman always left his audience desiring more.

"Where are you keeping her?" Carmichael asked Povetkin, once they both had feet on terra firma, a mechanic hovering around the two-man chopper, making sure that it was ready to depart upon command.

"She's in the bungalow, downstairs," Povetkin said. "Eddie and Tony had her stashed in Brooklyn, but I had them bring her here until the handoff."

"So, the ransom payment's on in spite of all that's happened, then?"

"Until we know the senator intends to cheat us beyond any doubt," the Russian said.

"And you don't think he's done that yet?" Carmichael asked. "Sending a team of mercenaries after us, for God's sake?"

"Think of that as an emotional reaction," said Povetkin. "Like a temper tantrum. How would you react at first, if someone snatched your child and threatened him or her with harm?"

Carmichael let that pass. He had two children, each by different mothers—floozy "stars" or his aboveboard porn productions, neither one acknowledged in his name, although he had supported each of them until they turned eighteen and could not pester him with any further legal claims. As for the mothers, one had overdosed on heroin in 1998; the other was a plumber's wife in Philadelphia and long since gone to seed.

If either child had been abducted, held for ransom, Carmichael supposed he would have let them die and changed his phone number to ward off any future calls from greedy strangers.

"And Rizzo's coming here?" Carmichael asked Povetkin, as they reached the backdoor of the Russian's manor house.

"Already on his way," Shamil replied. "He should be here within the hour. We can monitor the ransom drop from here. Find out if Maddox has recovered from his fit of pique and wishes to be sensible."

"And if he hasn't?"

They were in the kitchen now, its space and sparkling new equipment adequate to run a fair-sized restaurant.

"Then we proceed and shoot the film," Povetkin said. "I always keep my word."

"You figure that will stop the old man hiring guns to hunt us down?"

"A politician in your country lives on deference from those around him. Common people cast their votes for him based on the lies he tells them. Rich men in the shadows donate to a candidate who promises them favors and delivers. Neither group appreciates a man who steps outside the law too publicly, inviting scandal, an arrest and prosecution."

"But the heat that falls on him—"

"Cannot endanger us," Povetkin said. "Only one person living now knows all the secrets of our game, and if she speaks against us now she has as much to lose as anyone."

"That's if she's stable and her nerve holds up," Carmichael said.

Povetkin shrugged. "If it does not, she might become a movie star herself," he said. "Can you imagine that?"

Carmichael could…and wondered whether he was in the presence of a lunatic.

Passaic County, New Jersey

Angelo Rizzo's mini-convoy, three black SUVs, had left the Bronx via the George Washington Bridge, followed the New Jersey Turnpike to the I-80 Express Lane until it rolled through Elwood Park, and then southwest from there along the Garden State Parkway to Clifton. Rizzo, riding in the back of the lead vehicle, between two burly *soldati*, watched the dark landscape unfold and wished their trip was done.

Settimo Abbandando, Rizzo's chief lieutenant, swiveled in the forward shotgun seat and said, "We're almost there, Boss."

"I know where we are, Fingers," Rizzo replied, using the nickname that had stuck with Abbandando since he was a teenage pickpocket. His aide shrugged, faced back toward the SUV's windshield, their high-beam headlights burrowing a tunnel through the Jersey night.

The last thing Rizzo had expected or desired tonight was an alert from Brighton Beach that there had been an upset in the Maddox operation. Worse yet was the kind of upset that Shamil Povetkin had reported: three low-ranking members of the network missing at the very time when Harlan Maddox had a team of mercenaries in the field, trying to track his missing daughter down.

So here was Rizzo, riding through the night with body-guards surrounding him, instead of lying up at home with some showgirl, maybe a couple of them, trying to forget that they were only hours out from the appointed ransom drop, no clear idea of what was happening or how the deal had seemingly begun to fall apart.

He didn't mind losing the small fry, even though replacing them would be a royal pain in the *culo*. Vetting new participants took time and more than just the usual discretion that was used for screening workers in an outlaw gaming room, for instance, or a waterfront protection racket. With the snuff trade—and a U.S. senator's daughter no less—the stakes went through the roof, along with the prospective payoff.

Harlan Maddox, Rizzo understood, was not so different from himself. He had accumulated wealth and power through a long, hard slog and relished wielding both against his enemies in government and private life. Rizzo knew that the senator would never, ever give up tracking down the individuals responsible for his sole daughter's death and degradation, any more than Rizzo would have, if he'd had a child.

While Maddox lived, reprisal was a clear and present danger. But eliminating him, while possible, would be equivalent to playing hot potato with a live grenade. The job would have to be done perfectly, no botched attempts or second chances, and the heat that it provoked would linger on for years.

Hell, people were still yammering about who killed the Kennedys back in the Sixties, and that furor showed no signs of letting up, although the plotters had issued deathbed confessions twenty years after the fact.

Settimo Abbandando, after being scolded once, did not announce that they had reached Shamil Povetkin's country hideaway-com-studio. Rizzo, who'd visited the Russian in New Jersey half a dozen times, immediately recognized the stone wall on his right, the wrought-iron gates manned by a pair of heavies who revealed no weapons but would have them ready, somewhere close at hand.

The *bratva* soldiers loved their submachine guns and assault rifles, mostly produced in Mother Russia, sold by millions to all kinds of terrorists around the world, regardless of political philosophies. Money spoke loudest with the former Communists, and their elected president—a former KGB man who had "seen the light" in 1991 and scrambled into bed with mobsters faster than a cheap call girl—maintained the capitalist oligarchy with a rod of iron, eliminating anyone who criticized his government by means of prison terms or murder.

He was Rizzo's kind of guy—which didn't mean that Angelo trusted Shamil Povetkin any farther than he could have thrown the Russian's manor house one-handed.

If the Maddox operation blew up in their faces, Rizzo planned to hold Povetkin privately responsible and make him pay for it in blood.

But not tonight, he hoped.

They still had time, a chance to save the plan, and if it worked…well, they could even think about a rerun, somewhere down the line.

But first, they absolutely had to deal with Harlan Maddox's hit team, wipe them off the map for good.

Beginning now.

"You think your daddy cares about you?"

Carrie Maddox didn't bother answering the question from the weasel who had spiked her cocktail at The Red Zone and abducted her. She still knew him as "Devon," but had heard his pimply sidekick—"Tony," no last name—refer to him as "Eddie" when they talked, apparently not caring if she heard their given names.

That worried Carrie. She had seen enough movies and TV shows about kidnapping that she understood two basic facts. Abductors who had given any thought to letting victims walk away unharmed, once ransom had been paid, took care to hide their faces and avoid using each other's names within earshot of hostages.

A captive who had seen their faces and/or heard their names, as Carrie had, immediately shifted from the role of victim to potential prosecution witness, and the penalties for ransom kidnapping were strict—a minimum of twenty years in federal prison with no prospect of parole, or execution if a death resulted from the snatch.

When Carrie did not answer Devon/Eddie's taunting question, he edged closer to her, scraping the plastic foot caps on his metal folding chair's legs squeaking on concrete. Behind him, sitting off to one side, Tony wore a sly smile on his acne-ravaged face.

"You still don't get it, do you?" Eddie/Devon asked, prodding her rib cage with a bony index finger, nail chewed to the quick.

God, Carrie thought. *How did I ever think this piece of shit was "cute"?*

The only answer she could think of: she'd been well along her way to drunk before she's met him at The Red Zone and he'd spiked her drink with whatever it was he used. It sickened her to think she might have asked him back to her dorm room for sex, unaware he was intent on drugging and abducting her.

Never again, she thought, and almost laughed aloud at that, considering the fact that she had no hope of escaping her predicament.

That must have shown on Carrie's face, since Eddie frowned at her and said, "You think this is a joke, bitch? That your daddy's gonna float some cash and you'll go back to how things were before? How stupid *are* you, huh?"

She didn't answer, but that was not stopping him. Leering, he said, "I hate to break it to you, darlin', but somebody close to you at home don't want you coming back. This whole thing was a setup from the get-go in your own backyard."

Tony giggled at that, repeating "In your own backyard" as if he were a parrot.

"You're a liar," Carrie said, wishing she could have mustered more conviction.

"Am I?" Eddie leaned in toward her, gave her breast a tweak that made her skin crawl, even if she couldn't scoot beyond his reach. "Let's think about who might be sick and tired of you, wanting you gone. A party girl who's nearly flunking out of school, flushing your daddy's hard earned graft down the crapper?"

Carrie's cheeks were burning as she listened to him, wishing she could silence him, but sensing that there was at least some truth in what he said. Of course, her father had been gravely disappointed in her lately, and she couldn't bear to think of how her mother might be feeling, if she'd been alive. As for Jolene...

The best that she could manage, facing Eddie from a yard away, was telling him, "You're full of shit!"

He laughed at her, then slapped her face. "Just like I thought," he said. "You're dumb as dirt. Who's gonna miss you when you're gone?"

Between the slap and Eddie's words, Carrie could not prevent hot tears from spilling down her cheeks. "You'll die in prison," she retorted, knowing that it sounded lame. "The both of you."

"Not us, sweetheart," Eddie replied. "We got protection, see? We're covered."

"Tell that to your executioners at supermax, scumbag," she answered back.

This time, instead of slapping her, Eddie reared back and punched her in the face, topping the chair that she was duct-taped into, slamming Carrie down onto the concrete floor. She felt blood flowing from her nostrils as she lay there, stunned.

"Jesus, man!" Tony blurted at his associate. "The man sees that mess, I ain't taking any heat for it."

"Shut up," Eddie replied, but with a tremor in his voice as if he knew he'd gone too far. "She's got a whole lot worse coming to her before we're done."

"Another wall," Reg Hardy said.

"At least no broken glass this time," Natalie Karpin answered.

"Nope. Just wrought-iron spikes," said Blake Mahoney.

They broke out the scaling ropes again and scattered from the point where they had stashed their rented cars in darkness, the Mahoney brothers moving toward the south side of Shamil Povetkin's property, while Hardy, Natalie and Stan Dartnell circled around to enter from the east.

Climbing Povetkin's wall was no great challenge, tossing nooses from the ground below over a nine-inch spike in each case, testing each to prove that they could bear a person's weight, then scrambling to the top in single file. The dicey part was trying to avoid a painful snag on any of the sharpened spines, after confirming that the nearest ground below was not patrolled by guards or dogs. With that achieved, it was an easy drop into the Russian's property, the last one over in each case bringing the rope along and stashing it in handy shrubbery.

So far, so good.

Advancing on the house required more stealth. Lights shone from windows on the mansion's first and second floors, while floods suspended from the eaves in back picked out the mini-helicopter that had borne Povetkin and Joel Carmichael to New Jersey while the Russian's men were going down in Brighton Beach. No guard had been assigned to watch the chopper, but three men were stationed on the patio in back, drifting around the redbrick barbecue and swimming pool with automatic weapons on display.

"No getting past them quietly," Hardy observed.

"We'll need to make it quick instead," Grant said.

"And take the Zefhir out," Blake added, "so they can't give us the slip again."

The point where they had rallied gave the team a visual

beyond the house, around its south wing, toward Grove Street and sprawling cemetery opposite. As they stood watching from the shadows, three black SUVs pulled up and stopped before the wrought-iron gate out front, guards hastening to roll the barrier aside and wave the new arrivals through, then close the gate again when all had passed inside.

"More company," Dartnell said, as the vehicles rolled out of sight along Povetkin's paved driveway.

They could not see the SUVs once they'd drawn closer to the house, but heard doors slamming as their occupants piled out. Someone called out a greeting to the new arrivals, answered by a spokesman for the drop-ins.

"So, the more the merrier," Blake said.

"Figure another dozen guns," Natalie estimated. "Minimum."

"Another partner in the racket," Grant suggested. "What we need is someone who can steer us to wherever they've stashed Carrie Maddox."

"And sufficient time to make whoever that is spill his guts," Hardy amended.

"I can do the 'copter," Dartnell offered. "Yank a few wires and its done."

"Okay," Grant said. "The rest of us will cover you and then move in together. Keep those photos of Carmichael and Povetkin clear in mind, for when it goes to hell."

Because that was inevitable, sure. In the 1870s, Helmuth von Moltke, Chief of Staff for Prussia's army, had expressed a fact that every soldier on the planet recognized throughout the span of human history: *No plan survives first contact with the enemy.* That had been true when Ice Age cavemen fought with clubs, and it was true today.

A soldier who did not anticipate the unexpected was as good as dead.

Dartnell ran toward the helicopter while his teammates started toward Povetkin's home away from home. Reaching the small aircraft, he opened up one of its doors and started ripping wires loose from the instrument panel. Significant repairs would be required to get the whirlybird airborne again, and in the meantime, anyone who tried to flee the property would have to use the gate facing Grove Street, exposed to hostile fire.

Leaving the Curti Zefhir useless, Dartnell followed the remainder of his team toward the rear entrance of Shamil Povetkin's house. Before he caught up to the others, gunfire sputtered in the spacious home's backyard, the guards surprised and dropping before they could mount an adequate defense.

Three were out of action, with an unknown number still inside the house or out in front, greeting at least a dozen reinforcements just arriving on the scene. The odds were poor, but Stan had beaten worse since joining the Mahoney team—and even earlier, when he was serving with his homeland's Special Operations Command, including a 2003 raid on the North Korean freighter MV *Pong Su*, caught unloading heroin valued at $160 million in Australian waters. Four members of the crew pled guilty while in custody, but Dartnell had been disappointed when their "penalty" was limited to deportation, even though the confiscated ship was later sunk by laser-guided bombs.

Win some, lose some.

But if his side should lose tonight, Stan reckoned none of them were going home alive.

13

Joel Carmichael was standing with Shamil Povetkin as the three black SUVs rolled through the Russian's gates and drew up to a halt before the mansion's broad front porch. Angelo Rizzo followed one of his gorillas from the backseat of the first crew wagon, chewing a cigar and scowling as he joined them on the porch, his other gunmen fanning out around the cars.

No greeting from the mafioso, just a curt demand for information from their host. "So, what in hell is going on you couldn't tell me on the phone, Shamil."

Povetkin forced a smile and said, "Please, come inside where we can speak in private, eh?"

"Bad news again," Rizzo predicted. "If you couldn't guess, I'm getting sick and tired of this."

"And yet, we must discuss it all the same," Povetkin said, turning to lead the way inside his spacious second home.

"Yeah, yeah," The Animal replied. "Let's get it done already."

They had barely crossed the threshold when a rattling sound like fireworks sounded from somewhere behind the house. Carmichael recognized the echo of gunfire and stopped dead in his tracks, one foot across Povetkin's threshold.

"Shit!" As Rizzo cursed, he drew a pistol from beneath his jacket, gripping it with muzzle pointed toward the entry's parquet flooring. "What's *this* now?"

Povetkin tried to keep his cool and nearly managed it. "My men can handle anything," he said, trying to reassure his guests—and possibly himself. "We're safe inside the house."

"This ain't a bunker, Shammy," Rizzo answered back. His gun began to rise. "You drop me into something here, I swear to God you'll never live to laugh about it with your buddies from the KGB."

One of Povetkin's soldiers, standing by, leveled an automatic weapon at the mafioso's chest and barked something in Russian, before Shamil stepped between his man and Rizzo, hands raised shoulder-high. "Stop this," he urged. "We have a common enemy who will rejoice if we begin to kill each other now."

"What common enemy is that?" Rizzo demanded, while he kept his sidearm pointed at Povetkin's man.

"It's what I called you to discuss," Povetkin answered. "The mercenaries hired by Harlan Maddox."

"Christ! The guys I warned you two about just yesterday?"

"It seems they have been making better progress than we hoped."

"We?" Rizzo fairly sneered at him.

"This is no time for blaming one another," Shamil said. "If they are here now—"

"*If?*" Another burst of automatic gunfire punctuated Rizzo's question, right on cue.

"We can eliminate them," said Povetkin. "Tell the senator that his betrayal means a doubling of the ransom first demanded."

"Screw that!" Rizzo said, already moving backwards toward the open door and his three SUVs. "I'm clearing outa here while I still can."

"But Angelo—"

A sound of bullets smashing glass somewhere behind them, from the general direction of Povetkin's kitchen and his formal dining room, cut off the Russian's words.

"He's leaving now?" Carmichael asked, incredulous. "Just

driving off and leaving us?"

"*Zabud' o nem!*" Povetkin snapped. "Forget about him! We must get away from here while time remains."

Carmichael saw his host turn toward the sound of battle emanating from the mansion's rear, striding away from him.

"You're going *toward* the shooting?" he challenged.

"I am," Povetkin answered. "And unless you wish to die tonight, you're coming with me. Now!"

Reg Hardy followed Natalie Karpin around the north side of the manor house while the Mahoney brothers jogged off to the south. A glance back toward Shamil Povetkin's mini-helicopter showed Stan Dartnell finished there, making a beeline for the mansion's sliding glass doors facing on the patio.

Divide and conquer, or split up and die piecemeal?

It was too damned late to second-guess their battle plan at this point. Reinforcements rolling up out front lengthened the odds against survival, but the SFX team had already come too far to turn back now.

Behind him, as Hardy and Karpin turned the corner, he heard Dartnell fire a burst of 5.56mm rounds to clear the sliding doors, glass raining down on top of paving stones like sheets of ice losing their hold on roofing shingles when the sun shines. Hardy wished Stan luck inside the Russian's house and left him to it, focusing on Natalie and what they'd face when they emerged in front.

Before they reached that destination, though, a pair or Russian shooters dashed around the mansion's northwest corner, intercepting them. Reg recognized them at a glance from their tattoos, extending from their short collars to illustrate their cheeks, a *bratva* trait that would have worked against them if they weren't too arrogant to strive for subtlety.

The soldiers pulled up short at sight of Reg and Natalie approaching them, their automatic weapons rising into line for snap shots from the hip. Nat was a split-second ahead of Hardy, triggering a three-round burst from her M4 and taking down the Russian on their right, his slack form tumbling over backwards through a crimson mist.

Reg followed with a short bust of his own, stitching a line of holes across the second shooter's chest and dropping him beside his comrade on the bloodstained grass. They pushed on past the twitching corpses, toward the spacious lawn and driveway trailing off toward Grove Street in the middle distance, getting there just as the three black, late-arriving SUVs were revving up in preparation to depart again.

The wagons—one Toyota 4Runner, two Ford Lincoln Aviators—hadn't taken on their crews yet, but were in the process, drivers in their seats and five or six guys dressed in shiny suits standing around each vehicle with weapons drawn, watching for handy targets. None of the faces popped for Hardy, but he guessed that state and local cops would recognize most of them from their various arrest and prison records.

While the shooters hadn't spotted any marks to fire on yet, they seemed intent on covering one hulking figure Hardy took to be their boss—a bullet-headed, greasy-haired palooka who reminded Reg of every movie "godfather" he'd ever seen, what Old World Mafiosi called "a man with a belly" to showcase respect.

"Looks like a boss to me," said Natalie, her M4 carbine up and shouldered as she marked her target through the weapon's Aimpoint sight. A red dot showed up on the runner's back, around the beltline and a bit off center as she squeezed the carbine's trigger and a 5.56mm boat-tail bullet cracked down range.

The rifle bullet struck Angelo Rizzo just above his right hip, tearing through what snippy chick-lit writers would have called his "love handle," and ripped a fist-sized exit wound in front, soaking his wool slacks made in Italy for Saks Fifth Avenue with spurting blood.

The Animal was falling, would have hit the driveway's asphalt with a tragic faceplant, but a pair of his *soldatos* caught him by his arms and held him upright, more or less, telling Rizzo that he wasn't hit too badly as they dragged him toward the black Toyota's gaping left-rear door. His other men were cursing, firing all around him, seemingly without a clear-cut target, as his would-be saviors hoisted him into the SUV's backseat, assisted by another goombah who had entered from the right-hand side to drag their boss inside.

"You're gonna be okay, Boss," one of them was saying, clearly bullshit from the fact that Rizzo's whole right side was going numb, maybe a sign of shock, or else an indicator that he was already bleeding out.

"*Vaffanculo!*" he snapped at no one in particular, even as his mind registered the effort behind made to save him. Wishing he'd worn Kevlar underneath his tailored suit tonight, Rizzo was moved to wonder if his troops were already too late.

One of his soldiers, nicknamed Icepick for the old-school murder weapon that he favored, gave a little coughing noise and seemed to barf in Rizzo's face. It took another second for The Animal to realize it wasn't bile, but rather blood, spraying from Icepick's ruptured face, another exit wound that dropped him like a sack of dirty laundry on the driveway's concrete apron.

Head shot.

Under other circumstances, Rizzo might have hit the backseat's floorboard, ducking down to save himself from any further injury, but he could feel hot blood and the remains of supper—minestrone soup and pasta primavera—pulsing from his ruptured abdomen into his lap.

If Rizzo wasn't dying, this would do until the real thing finally caught up with him.

"Come on, let's go!" his driver, Benny Catalano, shouted from his place behind the Lincoln's steering wheel. The SUV was rolling out as two of Rizzo's men piled in on either side of him, bracing him upright, after one of them dragged Icepick's faceless body from the left-rear doorway. One more dropped into the shotgun seat, and they were on their way back toward the wrought-iron gate on Grove Street, peeling out before the Lincoln's could catch up.

Rizzo was trying to work out the mileage to the nearest hospital—Saint Nary in Clifton, he thought it was, on East Madison Avenue—but focusing his thoughts was growing harder by the second. Slumped back on the bloodstained bench seat, Rizzo felt his mind spinning, like it was circling a toilet bowl or getting ready to evacuate his skull entirely.

By the time he realized that he was slipping into darkness, passing out, The Animal was gone.

Stan Dartnell wasn't on his own inside Shamil Povetkin's man-or house. Clearing the kitchen, he could hear men running here and there, shouting to one another in Russian, and while that was not one of the five languages that he spoke, the back-and-forth told Stan that anyone he met in there would be an enemy.

And he would deal with them accordingly.

The next room to the kitchen was a formal dining room, its table long enough and with sufficient chairs to comfort-ably welcome twenty diners. Dartnell had a feeling it was rarely used for meetings of that size and didn't care. The two men waiting for him in that lavish setting were enough for him to handle at the moment.

They were headed his way, almost certainly responding to the backyard sounds of gunfire, but appeared surprised to actually meet an adversary in the house. Both carried variations of the classic AK-47, one a stubby AKS-74U, the other possibly an AK-101 or AK-107.

Whatever they were, the Russians never had a chance to use them. Dartnell caught them gaping at him, shocked to find him there, and triggered two short M4 bursts before they got their AKs into action. Firing at the *soldat* on his right first, he put three rounds in the ten ring, center mass, and slammed the target over on his back, a little "woof" of impact driven from his dying lungs.

That stalled the second shooter, with the larger weapon, long enough for Stan to rotate five degrees or so and fire again. That time, his 5.56mm bullets found their mark about eight inches higher, shattering the Russian's lower face and spinning him around, an awkward pirouette that sprayed blood on the wall beside him in an abstract pattern as he fell.

Five down that he was sure of now, counting the gunmen on the patio out back—and how many remaining to defend Povetkin's hideaway? Had any of the tardy reinforcements come inside, or were they still out front, unloading from their SUVs? The only way that he could tell was to proceed, forging ahead.

And if he met Shamil Povetkin or Joel Carmichael some-where along the way, Stan had some questions one or both of them would have to answer.

Not that it would save their rotten lives.

He wouldn't mention that first thing, of course. Better to offer an interrogation subject hope, however slim, to start a useful dialogue. Allow the pigeon to believe he might escape the final judgment that was coming to him, if he only told the truth, confessed, pretending that he'd found his conscience and revived it after all these years.

Jabbering voices—Russian—put him on alert and wiped Stan's thoughts of what might happen if he stumbled on to either of the SFX team's primary targets. So far he had used no more than one-third of the M4 carbine's magazine, no reason to waste precious micro-seconds swapping for a full one now.

The voices told him he would next be facing two more soldiers, maybe three, and Stan reckoned that he could handle that.

And if he couldn't…well, the party had to end sometime, somehow.

Shamil Povetkin left his hideout through a side door that his enemies had either overlooked or hadn't reached yet, Joel Carmichael trailing closely on his heels. They ran in tandem past the dead *soldaty* sprawled out on his patio and past the swimming pool, reaching the Curti Zefhir two-seat helicopter without being challenged anywhere along the way.

Shamil was thankful that he'd taken flying lessons after his arrival in the States, avoiding the requirement that he hire a pilot who might let him down in an emergency such as the one in which he found himself right now. That also would have meant buying a larger aircraft, when the Zefhir on its own sold for a cool $1 million, a single-engine Eurocopter EC120 Colibri Hummingbird five-seater piled another $700,000 onto that.

Reaching the mini-copter, Shamil popped the pilot's door and settled in at the controls before he noticed something wrong. A snarl of insulated wires had been ripped loose from the Zefhir's control panel and grazed against his leg now, like the tentacles of an emaciated, multi-colored octopus.

Povetkin stopped short of trying to start the chopper's Velká Bíteš turboshaft engine, knowing that it would not respond and might in fact be rigged somehow to detonate if Shamil pressed the starter button. He was cursing bitterly in Russian when Carmichael piled into the cockpit's second seat, eyes dropping to the damage someone had inflicted on their best means of escape.

"Shit!" the producer blurted out. "What's this?"

"Somebody does not want us leaving, *pridurok*."

Povetkin doubted whether his companion understood the Russian word for "moron," but Carmichael clearly picked up on his tone, flinching as if he feared Shamil might backhand him. "So what are we supposed to do?" he asked, still cringing.

"We are supposed to die," Povetkin answered, "if our adversaries have their way. But we are not defeated yet."

"Oh, no? What have you got in mind before the credits roll? You want to hop the walls you built around this place and make a break for it on foot?"

Povetkin sneered at Carmichael. "How did you live this lone, being so foolish?"

"Hey, now!"

"*Zatknis'!*" the Russian snapped. "Shut up and listen!"

His companion, almost pouting, did as he was told.

"Now," Shamil forged ahead, "you may remember that I have several cars garaged here. If we reach them—"

"If?"

Povetkin drew a pistol from beneath his jacket, thrust its muzzle toward Carmichael's face. "You interrupt me once more time, *mudak*, and I will silence you for good."

Carmichael raised his hands, a signal of abject surrender.

"Better," said Shamil, and let his weapon drop until it pointed at Carmichael's groin. "Now, *when* we reach the cars, I drive us out of here and we are safe. I have no end of bolt-holes set up for emergencies."

"And what about the girl?" Carmichael asked, a tremor in his voice.

"Don't worry," said Shamil. "I'll give instructions while we're on our way. Come now, before it is too late."

Natalie Karpin's voice stopped Grant Mahoney in his tracks, as he and brother Blake approached the Grove Street frontage of Shamil Povetkin's home.

"The target's lost his reinforcements," she announced, over the Bluetooth link the SFX team members shared. "They're bugging out."

Blake heard the message simultaneously, stopping short. Out front, the crackle of small arms fire faltered for a moment, while the sound of revving motors rose, then gained more distance from the house, retreating toward the street a hundred yards away.

"Could you I.D. who's running?" Grant inquired over the air.

"No sign of either mark we came in looking for," Natalie answered back.

So, no Shamil Povetkin. No Joel Carmichael III.

"They're either in the house," Blake said, "or looking for another exit."

Stan Dartnell's voice, disembodied, joined the dialogue. "Forget the chopper," he advised. "It isn't going anywhere tonight."

"But they won't know that," Grant surmised. "It brought them here. They'd try escaping that way first."

Blake frowned. "And failing that?" he asked.

"Can't say," said Grant. "We'd better check it out."

A nod from Blake, and Grant informed the rest, "We're falling back to check around behind the house. Satellite photos have some structures back there that could cover rolling stock, workshops, whatever."

"Right behind you," Hardy chimed in a split-second later.

Natalie concurred with, "Copy that!"

"I've got another floor to cover," Dartnell said, "before I call it quits inside the house."

"Just watch your six," Grant cautioned the Australian.

"Always do," Stan said, then cut the link.

Their Google Earth satellite photos of Povetkin's Jersey hideaway had not provided any information on what lay beneath the roofs of various outbuildings on the Russian's property. One seemed to be the proper size for a three-car garage, which made sense if Povetkin traveled overland from Gotham to the Garden State, instead of flying in. Another building, farther from the mansion, could have been a three-

or four-room bungalow, purpose unknown. The rest were smaller, tool sheds and the like, where frightened men might hide, but offering no prospect for escape.

"Figure they're armed," Blake said, as he retraced their steps with Grant. "The Russian, anyway."

"No way to tell which one of them can point the way to Carrie Maddox though," Grant said. "We need to count on taking both alive."

Grant did not voice his worst fear, that the snuff purveyors might not know precisely where Carrie was stashed, or even whether she was still alive. In that event, scorched earth would be the only option left to them, and without bringing Carrie Maddox home, he'd count the mission as a failure.

They came around the mansion's southwest corner and immediately saw two figures running from the helicopter Dartnell had disabled, toward the largest or the spacious property's outbuildings.

"When you're right, you're right, bro," Blake allowed.

Grant recognized the runners from their photos, fired a warning shot into the night from his M4 carbine, and shouted to them, "Stop right there!"

14

Joel Carmichael heard the shout of "Stop right there!" and froze dead in his tracks. Some twenty feet in front of him and that much nearer the garage, Shamil Povetkin also halted, turning toward the sound.

Both fleeing men immediately saw two strangers closing on them from the southwest corner of Povetkin's house, both dressed in black and carrying assault rifles, with pistols holstered on their belts, their matching battle vests replete with pouches holding extra magazines to feed their guns. Carmichael noted a resemblance in their faces, but beyond that knew them only as a pair of nameless enemies.

Povetkin spoke before Carmichael found his voice, if he had dared to say a word with automatic weapons pointed at him.

"Who are you?" Shamil demanded. "And what do you want?"

"We're after Carrie Maddox," one of the pair said. "To take her home."

"I don't know who that is," Povetkin lied. "What makes you think I know where you can find her?"

Closer know, the older-looking of the riflemen replied, "We have a lock on how you make your money and we're not accepting any bullshit. Give her up right now. Last chance."

"Ah," said Povetkin, stalling. "So you are the mercenaries who the senator believes can challenge me?"

Carmichael felt as if the oxygen had been extracted in a heartbeat from the night air that surrounded him. He saw a subtle movement of Povetkin's hand toward his waistband, although if he could see it, Joel supposed it might not be so subtle after all.

"I'm counting down," the seeming younger of their adversaries said. "On three you die. Two."

"Wait!" Carmichael blurted out, his voice rasping like sandpaper. "Where was 'two'?"

"It slipped my mind," the scowling rifleman replied.

Before he had a chance to utter "three," Povetkin finished reaching for the pistol tucked under his belt, drew it, and started raising it to fire, knees flexing as he ducked into a crouch.

Both automatic rifles spoke as one, a single shot from each. Povetkin vaulted backwards, sprawling on the grass with arms outflung and gasping from the impact of two bullets in his chest. The pistol tumbled from his hand as the invaders of his property advanced to stand above him.

"Well, that's unfortunate," the older-looking of them said.

"His call," the second rifleman replied, emotionless.

A rattling sound emerged from Shamil's throat and ruptured lungs before his body slackened and lay still.

Both rifles swung toward Carmichael, making him flinch involuntarily.

"I hope you're smarter than your friend here," said the shooter to his right.

"I hope so too," Carmichael answered, nearly whispering.

"So, can you point us to the girl or not?" the other asked.

"We're all in luck," Carmichael said, knowing his life might only last while he was useful to these executioners. "She's here!"

"Show us," the elder of them said. "And make it quick."

"A filming studio, you said?" asked Grant Mahoney. "Right here at his house?"

"The land's not in Povetkin's name," Carmichael answered as they trailed him through the darkness. "I'm surprised you found us here."

"We have our ways," Blake said. "This better not be crap."

Grant had already signaled to the other members of their team over the hidden Bluetooth microphone, alerting them to disengage and form up at their destination at the east end of Povetkin's property as soon as feasible. Acknowledgements told him the others were in motion, nearly finished mopping up.

Behind them, toward Grove Street, the sounds of gunfire had begun to peter out. Next up, Grant figured, would be sirens wailing in the early morning dark.

Carmichael jabbered on, as if to keep his nerve intact, his feet moving. "It's not the only place he films, of course. Wouldn't be safe full-time. But sometimes, when he's in a mood, he likes to watch and get...involved."

"Make that past tense," Grant said.

"Oh, right. So are you gonna kill me, too?" The question tightened up his vocal cords, reduced Carmichael's question to an anxious whisper.

Blake answered first. Said, "That depends on you."

"Right. Sure. I'm helping you."

"We'll be the judge of that," Grant said. "How many watchers staying with her?"

"Two," Carmichael said. "Unless they heard the racket and got spooked. They're not real soldiers."

"Fancy that," Blake said. "Just kidnappers and murderers?"

"Povetkin likes—um, *liked*—to call them talent scouts."

Neither Mahoney brother shared their captive's nervous laugh.

The bungalow-type building stood before them now, no windows visible, bearing only a vague resemblance to the structure caught on Google Earth by satellite photography.

"Who's in there with her?" Grant demanded.

"Eddie Rattigan," Carmichael said, "and Tony Gutierrez.

They switch off finding girls, or sometimes guys, depending on what Shamil has—or *had*—in mind for filming."

"Made to order, is it?" Blake inquired, clearly disgusted with their captive and the homicidal racket he had helped to operate.

"Could be," Carmichael said. "It's mostly girls, but for a special order from a VIP, you know, they'd have to front fifty percent."

"You have a list of customers?"

"*I* don't," said Joel. "The business end is all Shamil. He claims to have it backed up on computer somewhere, if he ever needs to bargain, but I couldn't swear that's true. It cuts both ways."

Grant let that go. Asked Carmichael, "These guys with Carrie. Are they armed?"

"Beats me," Joel said. "They keep an eye on girls they bring, feed them, like that. Might have a couple guns, I guess, but may not know what's happening."

"How's that?" Blake asked.

"The studio is soundproofed, right? First-class."

Grant felt an urge to shoot him there and then but managed to suppress it. "Have you got some kind of signal for approaching them?"

"You mean like code?"

"Like that."

"Not that I know of. There's a doorbell king of thing, flashes a light inside but doesn't chime. Povetkin didn't want some drop-in messing up the soundtracks."

"And these assholes know you?" Blake inquired.

"We've met a couple times. I keep that to a minimum, you know?"

They'd reached the so-called studio and stood before its only door, no peepholes visible. A button on the wall resembled any other doorbell, offering no hint of what might lie within. A speaker on the wall beside it trailed wires up and out of sight under the building's eaves.

"Okay," Grant told their prisoner. "Ring through."

"Sure thing," Carmichael said, then half-turned toward his captors. "But first, I guess there's something else you ought to know."

"Which is?" Grant asked.

"Who set this up," Carmichael said. "You'd never guess it in a million years."

Carrie Maddox saw the red light flashing in her cell—what her kidnappers called a "sound stage"—furnished with a thrift-store bed, legs bolted to the concrete floor, and an old wooden chair on which she how sat, one ankle shackled to its right-front leg.

The chair was also bolted down, her chain just long enough to reach the toilet in a tiny bathroom eight or nine feet from the bed, no sink in there to let her wash or even snatch a drink of water while she waited for whatever happened next.

She knew about the flashing red light. That meant some-one had arrived outside the building where she was confined and was demanding entry. Without knowing who that might be, what they wanted, Carrie understood that it could only be another enemy.

Who else would ring the bell instead of bursting through the door with battering rams?

She and her jailers, phony "Devon" and his partner Tony, were entirely unaware of any riotous disturbance on the grounds outside. The bungalow-cum-filming studio was soundproofed from its basement to its eaves and attic, or whatever lay above the ceiling of her cell. No one but her abductors had free access to the property, which Carrie—drugged, hooded and bound upon arrival, trapped inside a van whose racing engine was the only sound that reached her ears—had no reason to believe that anyone was likely to arrive and rescue her.

The first emotion that had died within her, after she regained full consciousness, was hope.

Each time before since she'd been shackled in this cell, the blinking red light meant some unseen visitor had brought another Swanson frozen dinner, microwaved but chilling by the time Devon or Tony brought it to her with an unwashed plastic spork.

This time, however, it was different.

She heard one of her captors tell the other, "Holy, shit! It's *him*." The other one's response was garbled, barely audible, but both were clearly agitated, but without an explanation as to why.

Carrie could only wait and wonder what would happen to her next.

"What in hell's Carmichael doing here?" asked Eddie Rattigan. "And who are those guys with him?"

Antonio Gutierrez frowned and shook his head. "Some of Shamil's soldiers, maybe?"

"They look Russian to you?"

"You're asking me, *ese*? Gringos all look the same, man."

"Dumbass."

"Says the dipshit asking questions. Better open up before you piss 'em off."

"Hang on a second." Rattigan studied the CCTV monitor where three men stood, two strangers flanking Joel Carmichael, whom they recognized. He eyed the automatic carbines they were carrying. Asked, "Why are they coming in heavy?"

"Did you ever see one of Povetkin's guys without a gun?"

"It doesn't feel right," Eddie answered, as he drew a pistol from his belt.

"Whoa, man!" Tony protested. "What are you—"

Carmichael's voice cut through his protest, sounding raspy and robotic through the intercom. "Goddamn it! Open up this door!"

Rattigan thought of answering, demanding that the men outside explain what they were after, but he lost that chance while trying to rev up his nerve.

One of the shooters flanking Carmichael elbowed Rattigan's boss aside and fired a three-round burst into the door, denting the sheet metal, dropping its shattered deadbolt on the concrete floor in front of Rattigan and Tony.

"*¡Jesucristo!*" Tony blurted, whipping a revolver from his shoulder holster, worn indoors without a jacket to conceal it. "*¿Qué carajo, hombre?*"

Eddie didn't speak his partner's lingo, but he got the gist of it. And he had no clue what in hell was happening right now.

"The girl, man! This ain't right. We need to guard her."

And he wasted no time shoving Tony toward the locked connecting door that stood between them and the Maddox woman's cell.

There was no other exit from that chamber, Eddie knew, but it was all that he could think of at the moment.

And what happened next was anybody's guess.

Blake Mahoney didn't feel like standing on the snuff film studio's doorstep and wasting precious time, when the gorillas holding Carrie Maddox captive might be taking steps to guarantee her silence on the far side of a bolted door. His M4 carbine burst removed that obstacle in record time, but simply charging past the threshold could be tantamount to suicide.

Wishing they had bought some stun grenades from Rocco Conti when they'd bought the Glocks and carbines, Blake knew there was no time now for do-overs or second-guessing. With a nod toward brother Grant, he grabbed a handful of Carmichael's jacket sleeve and tossed him through the gaping doorway into hell.

Who better to receive the first shots from his own men than the sick, depraved producer of the foulest "cinema" produced in any venue on the planet?

He survived for two or three seconds if that. A blaze of pistol fire erupted from the bungalow and Carmichael absorbed it, squealing as he vaulted backward through the doorway he'd just cleared, sprawling between the brothers on the studio's gray concrete porch, where some comedian had painted "WELCOME" and a cross-eyed smiley face with Devil horns.

Carmichael's blood soon covered that graffiti, while the two Mahoney's locked eyes with the open doorway in between them, hearing footsteps as the unseen shooters scurried to find cover.

Neither spoke audibly, but at a nod between them Blake crouched low and fired another short burst through the yawning entryway. Grant backed that up with six rounds of his own, then Blake ducked through the opening with Grant hot on his heels.

And saw no one.

They were in time to see another door slam shut and hear bolts being thrown inside the room beyond.

Could have been worse, Blake thought, noting the door was made of wood rather than steel, and thus not bulletproof unless the builders had anticipated an attack someday, spending a wad of cash to reinforce the other side against gunfire.

But if they fired through that last barrier, into the so-called studio, would they be putting Carrie's life at instant risk? Would one of her abductors try to use her as a hostage for their getaway?

Why not?

Grant also recognized that threat, miming directions to his brother as they crept up to the door's threshold. A couple of their rounds had already drilled peepholes through the wooden paneling, but anyone who tried to use them would be begging for a bullet in the head.

And what would Carrie's father do if he were present?

Pay somebody else to take the risks, no doubt, while watching from a safe remove. In fact, the very thing he had already done, trusting the SFX team to perform upon command and live up to their reputation with the feds.

So be it.

At his brother's nod, Blake leaned in toward the door, his carbine's muzzle brake mere inches from the last door's deadbolt and squeezed off another three-round burst.

Whatever happened next was in the hands of Fate.

Carrie Maddox huddled in the claustrophobic lavatory of her cell, the chain that linked one of her ankles to the wooden chair outside stretched taut across the floor. She could not halt the flow of tears that streaked her face and reckoned that she might pass out soon if she didn't find some way to regulate her panting breaths.

She did not wish to die here, in this room where she'd been caged, but saw no way around it now, with gunfire crashing in her ears.

The silent scream repeated in her mind, an endless loop: *Daddy, where are you?*

Nowhere to be found. Unless…

She heard the prick she'd known as "Devon"—Eddie now, apparently—telling his sidekick, "Find something to block the door!"

"Like what, *ese*?" the other bum replied. "The freaking furniture's all bolted down."

"Goddamn it!" Eddie snapped. "There must be something!"

"Point it out, you see it, man."

"Well, shit! How many rounds have you got left?"

"Three in the cylinder," said Tony. "Guess I used the rest on Carmichael."

"To hell with him. It's them or us now."

"Yeah, but—"

Tony never managed to complete his thought before the door blew inward, not like an explosion, but bullets tearing the locks apart in rapid fire. Carrie heard it but couldn't see the door directly from her hiding place, such as it was. She had to wonder how long she'd survive if shooting started in the creepy bedroom proper.

And that would be any second now.

Before that thought was even fully formed, the gunfire started up again, pistols against what she supposed must be some kind of submachine guns or assault rifles. Carrie knew nothing more about firearms than she had seen in action movies, but that was enough to tell her that when bullets filled the air, all kinds of people died or suffered grievous injuries. She'd seen the TV news reports about police who wound up killing hostages and bystanders instead of the perps they were shooting at, and now she had to wonder whether that would be her fate as well.

What could she do about it, either way?

And then, at that precise moment, Eddie the asshole found her cringing in the loo, reached down to gab one of her arms, and stuck his pistol in her face.

"Come on, bitch!" he commanded. "You're my ticket out of here!"

Fed up, she snapped and threw herself upon him, screaming, slapped his gun aside and wrapped both arms around his neck riding his back, fingernails raking Eddie's cheeks. It was his turn to scream then, cursing, flailing at her with the gun that couldn't seem to reach her lowered head, teeth fastened on his neck, as he lurched back into the noisy battle zone.

Grant Mahoney ducked low, threw himself into a shoulder roll across the threshold of a bedroom set for filming nightmares, and immediately landed in the midst of no man's land. His brother followed, standing up and with his M4 at the ready to confront their opposition.

Grant immediately saw two scruffy-looking younger men in front of him, both armed with pistols looking panicky and seeking cover as they fired wild shots at the intruders from a sparsely furnished bedroom which, he guessed, could double as a movie set if Carmichael and company were ready to replace the bloodstained furniture and repaint spattered walls each time.

There wasn't time to take an I.D. inventory of the hostile shooters beyond recognizing that they seemed to be two of a kind, your standard customers for late-night clubs where music threatened future hearing damage and the drinks were either watered down or spiked with date-rape drugs, their lives a waste at best, a threat to other citizens at worst.

Like now.

Grant saw no sign of Carrie Maddox in that moment, where his choices came down solidly on do or die. Carmichael had seemed certain she was somewhere in this bungalow, but the Mahoney brothers could not search the place if they were under fire.

A risk they'd clearly have to take.

Grant hit the closer of the two kidnappers—possibly Hispanic, with an untamed thatch of jet-black hair and eyes to match it—with a rising burst that punched three 5.56mm holes between his navel and his sternum, any one of them a sure-fire killer as the boat-tail bullets started tumbling on impact, tearing massive wound channels inside. The guy leapt backwards as if yanked out of the action by a giant stage hook from the days of vaudeville and landing faceup on the narrow bed.

Both brothers had the sole survivor pinned by Aimpoint red-dot sights when a young woman entered howling from their left and threw herself onto the gunman, wrapped her arms and legs around him—one slim ankle trailing rusty chain—and sank her teeth into his ear, the mouthful muffling her battle cry.

The guy went nuts, flailing around to free himself, wasting a shot that drilled acoustic ceiling tiles. Blake held his fire but stayed locked on their target, while Grant thumbed his M3's fire selector switch to semiauto, waiting for an opportunity to halt the mad swirling ballet.

Grant found his opening and stroked the carbine's trigger, saw his bullet drill a blood spout through the shooter's abdomen, Carrie Maddox and her final jailer sprawling in a wild tangle of limbs. While Blake moved in to separate them, telling Carrie they were emissaries from her father, Grant was on his Blue Tooth giving orders.

"Listen up! We've got her. Seems okay. Break off. Fall back on quadrant four asap and let's get out of here!"

15

The Majestic, Central Park West

A rough approximation of the group that had convened at Foley Square, less than two days before, had gathered in the posh apartment occupied by Harlan Maddox and his wife Jolene. The senator's daughter, after a checkup by the family's physician, was holed up in one of the co-op's spare bedrooms, out of sight and earshot from the rest. Physicians at Mount Sinai Hospital had checked her out, treated some minor injuries and gave the green light for bed rest at home.

Jolene Maddox was new to the assemblage, while its number from their first sit-down had been reduced by five. The SFX team's members in attendance, Grant Mahoney and Natalie Karpin, would report back to the other three when their outstanding business was concluded with the senator. Also missing from day one were Dwayne Ralston from the DOJ's Office of Legislative Affairs and NYPD Chief of Intelligence Carmine Alesio, their services and input no longer required. Still hanging in there were FBI Assistant Director in Charge Harold Duchene, Deputy Assistant U.S. Attorney Adele Wainwright, and NYPD Chief of Detectives Liam Byrne.

Their various assignments, on the backside of a hectic rescue mission, was delivering sitreps to Maddox and his missus, wrapping up the package with a somewhat less than tidy bow on top.

G-man Duchene and Liam Byrne began by summarizing what had gone down overnight, both carefully pretending that they didn't know the SFX team was involved. Since they had rubber-stamped the senator's approach to rescuing his daughter, neither of them was about to implicate himself in any aspect of the violence that had ensued. Their rival agencies had been familiar with Shamil Povetkin and Angelo Rizzo, both deceased now, but neither could explain how both had missed the two mobsters' involvement in the brutal underground of snuff films. Hal Duchene came closest to a weak apology, admitting that the Bureau planned on "reexamining its view" on such productions, without granting any future plans for an all-out investigation.

"What about this Carmichael?" asked Harlan Maddox of the room at large. He spoke the name as if it left a foul taste on his tongue. "Was no one keeping track of him at all?"

Neither the FBI nor NYPD would admit to any knowledge of the man behind the cameras, although Chief Byrne ran down the records of Carmichael's late associates Bennett, Yablonsky and Báez. Again, how they had dropped the ball on busting any of the three remained a mystery.

"Our best guess," Ralston from the DOJ chimed in, "is that they had some kind of line to City Hall, maybe in Albany, but as to who their cronies may have been…" He let the comment trail away, shrugging, and wound up staring at his shoes.

"So," Harlan Maddox said by way of summing up, "we really don't know any more than when we started, then?"

"Senator," Duchene replied, "we're confident that all the major players have been taken off the board." His eyes avoided Grant's and Natalie's.

"But not by any of your 'special' agents," Maddox said. "You still cannot identify the other victims of these savages, or even count them. You cannot assure us that some other gang of murderers aren't picking up where they left off right now."

"Senator—"

That was Grant Mahoney's cue, unknown to any other person in the sitting room, aside from Natalie.

"We did come up with something on another person who was active in the plot against your daughter, Senator," he said.

All eyes were on Mahoney now. Expressions on the faces turned his way ranged from bewilderment to shock. The lawmaker leaned forward, scowling, elbows planted on his knees.

"Ex*cuse* me?" he replied. "Another person?"

"It's the first I've heard of it," G-man Duchene chimed in.

"Same here," Chief Byrne added.

"All right," Senator Maddox said. "When were you planning to enlighten us?"

"We managed to debrief Carmichael," Grant replied, "before he had his accident last night."

"I feel a case of hearsay coming on," Adele Wainwright cautioned the room."

"Or you could say it was a dying declaration against interest," Ralston answered. "If it leads to anything, that is."

"I'm not a lawyer," Grant pressed on, "and I won't offer anybody here advice on what to do with what we learned. I've heard men talk while they were fading out, and some of them kept lying to the bitter end, no doubt. Others come clean. In my opinion, Carmichael was playing straight with us, still hoping that he might come out the other side with something left to build on."

"Very well, then," Harlan Maddox said. "By all means, fill us in."

Natalie answered that, beating Mahoney to the punch.

"I think," she said, "we'd better leave that to your wife."

From where Grant sat, he watched Jolene Maddox's face turn pale, the ghastly shade of ivory replaced a heartbeat later by two blooming ruddy blotches on her cheeks. It took another moment for her to recover, feeling all eyes in the room upon her now, before she could give voice to rage.

"Ask *me*?" she blurted out. "What's *that* supposed to mean? Who *is* the woman? What am I accused of?"

"I can break it down for you," Mahoney said, before the senator could get a handle on his voice. "Before he died, Carmichael filled us in on your affair with him, beginning when you lived in Hollywood."

"Jolene?"

She swiveled toward her husband, must have seen the doubt reflected on his face. "This is ridiculous, Harlan!" she said. "I've never heard such nonsense in my life."

"We've found a photograph of you and Carmichael to-gether," Grant replied. "Las Vegas, 1999, one of the annual hardcore award banquets the AVN coordinates."

The senator was glaring hard at Grant now. "AVN?" he challenged. "What on Earth is that?"

"The *Adult Video News*," Mahoney said. "Your wife and Carmichael were seated at a table near the stage, both smiling for the cameras."

"Is *that* all?" Jolene challenged him. "Harlan knows all about my film career. We have no secrets from each other."

"None?" Grant frowned at that. "Is he aware of your liai-sons at the Wyndham New Yorker Hotel, or at the Richmond Marriott back home?"

"Bullshit!" Jolene stormed back at him, dropping her usual reserved façade. "You're lying through your teeth, or else Carmichael was."

"He used his own name checking in at both hotels," Grant said. "No name provided for the lady who was with him."

"Well, then—"

"But the managers remembered you," Mahoney interrupted her. "Something they learn in training, I suppose. Never forget a face, especially the pretty ones."

"Jolene?" This time, when Harlan spoke, his famous voice had withered to a croak.

His wife wore a resolved face now, prepared to bluff it out.

"All lies," she told the room, then hedged. "I love my husband. Even if this tale you're spinning had an ounce of fact behind it, why would I conspire with anyone to harm a hair on Carrie's head?"

"*Suivez l'argent*," Grant said, one of the few phrases he still recalled from high school French, a class he'd only taken to meet girls.

"Which means?" G-man Duchene inquired.

"Follow the money," Grant translated for him. "Mrs. Maddox has been staring down the barrel of an iron-clad prenup since her wedding day."

"For God's sake!" Jolene interrupted him. "Is *that* your evidence? You think that I was planning a divorce from Harlan? Nothing could be further from the truth."

"I don't predict the future," said Mahoney, "but between your fling with Carmichael and your resentment of your husband's daughter with his late wife—"

"*What*? Who told you *that*?" Jolene demanded.

"Carrie's roommate at Columbia, for one," Grant said. Facing toward Harlan Maddox, he went on. "Your daughter didn't try to hide her feelings, Senator. I would imagine you've picked up on some of that yourself."

Maddox made no reply to that but his eyes shifted toward Jolene.

"Harlan," she said, "you can't be swallowing these lies."

"And then, Senator," Grant said, "there's the matter of your will."

Maddox could not control the flush of crimson rising in

his face. "That document is confidential," he protested. "If I find out that one of my lawyers has been telling tales, I'll have his ass disbarred."

"I haven't spoken to your law firm, sir," Grant said. "But Carmichael seemed to know the details of your will, chapter and verse, provided by your wife."

"Lie after lie!" Jolene cut in, her tone ramping for fury toward hysteria.

Grant shrugged. "How would I know, in that case, that the senator's estate is scheduled for an eighty-twenty split in Carrie's favor? Mrs. Maddox is provided for, of course—this co-op and enough to live on comfortably, severed if she takes another husband—but compared to the Virginia house and lands, the stock portfolio and all, that doesn't seem like much."

"Harlan?" Jolene turned to her spouse. "*Harlan*? You're not believing this?"

"But if your daughter predeceases both of you," Grant finished tying off the bow, the full estate belongs to Mrs. Maddox, plus her share of any ransom payment kicked back by her partners in the plan."

Jolene rose from the sofa, thrust her hands into the pockets of her night robe. "I simply *will not* sit and listen to these lies a second longer," she declared.

And when her right hand came back into view, it gripped a shiny pistol.

Pointed at her husband's startled face.

Jolene Maddox heard ringing in her ears, blood pressure spiking as her carefully constructed private world collapsed before her very eyes. Dressed in pajamas and a stylish robe, from which she'd drawn the .380-caliber Glock 28, now aimed directly at her husband's gaping maw.

She'd stuffed the little gun, weighing just twenty-four ounces with a loaded ten-round magazine, into her pocket on impulse, never supposing she would need it, even after all that had gone wrong so far. Now, facing six enemies in her parlor, with one more—her stepdaughter—sedated in a bedroom of their co-op, she supposed it must be Providence that put the notion in her mind.

Among the four men and two women facing her, Jolene supposed that only one, the FBI man, might be armed. It would require determination and some skill, but if she shot him first, the others seemed like relatively easy prey, and if she still could not devise some method of escape…well, there would be three shots remaining for herself.

How had it come to this?

She'd only wanted wealth, some time alone with Harlan before grief and age carried him off and left her sole heir to the family's fortune. Now, Jolene felt as if she were trapped inside that movie from the late Nineties, "A Simple Plan." It was almost enough to make her laugh out loud.

Almost.

But first, she had to save herself. And after that…

"Jolene? For Christ's sake!" Harlan said.

"Shut up!" she snapped at him, her index finger flexing slightly on the compact pistol's trigger, putting pressure on its automatic safety lever. "This is all your fault, the way you fawn over that spoiled brat, wasting money on her so-called education while she pisses it away and laughs behind your back. You never cared as much for me, not half as much!"

Some of the old familiar steel was back in Harlan's voice as he replied, "Carrie's my flesh and blood, Jolene."

"And what am I?" she raged at him, watching the others all the while. "Who do you think would nurse you through your final years? Your little party girl? Don't make me laugh!"

"No one's laughing, Jolene," one of the strangers said. The one who'd introduced himself as Grant Mahoney, proud of bringing down her orchestrated scheme in smoking ruins.

"Shut your mouth, damn you!" she snapped at him. "You're nothing but a criminal men like my husband hire to do their dirty work outside the law. What right do you have, judging me?"

"You've judged yourself," the mercenary said. "The only question now is whether you'll get out of here alive."

"A lot you care," she sneered. "You're just another weapon, like this one." And saying that, she jabbed the Glock's muzzle against her husband's forehead. "Point and squeeze."

"What did I ever see in you?" asked Harlan, moisture in his normally impassive eyes.

"You saw a woman twelve years younger than the one who died on you," she answered. "It's the oldest story in the Old Boy's book."

"And what does that make you, Jolene?"

"Exactly what you wanted, Harlan. Hot and willing in the sack, arm candy you could show off to your friends when you were in the mood."

G-man Duchene chimed in. "Think carefully about what happens next, Mrs. Maddox."

"Shut up and take your own advice," she answered. "Make a move and you'll be first to go, after this damned old fool."

"Jolene," her soon-to-be ex-husband said, "it's not too late."

"It is for you, old man."

Before her trigger finger could complete its follow-through, however, Harlan gripped her wrist in one strong hand and twisted it off-target. When she fired instinctively, the bullet missed his famous white coiffeur by fractions of an inch and tore into the sofa's cushions.

And before she had a chance to fire again, the woman who had come with Grant Mahoney—Natalie Something or Other—was in motion, springing from her chair, closing the gap between them in a fighting crouch, slamming a kick into Jolene's left knee that made her leg buckle beneath her.

Crying out, Jolene got off another shot into a nearby wall, her wrist still trapped in Harlan's grip. She saw one of the female mercenary's fists rushing to meet her face before the lights blinked out.

The rest was mopping up. Chief of Detectives Byrne phoned to NYPD's Central Park Precinct, ordering the watch commander to ignore any reports of a disturbance issuing from The Majestic. While he handled that, Harold Duchene put cuffs on Mrs. Maddox and disarmed her Glock, pulling its magazine, jacking a live round from its chamber, catching it in midair as it fell.

The would-be murderess was limp and unresponsive as her captors placed her on the couch her husband had already vacated, his face betraying stunned disgust at sharing space with her. Natalie Karpin checked Jolene's pulse, verified that she would come around in time, and granted that her dislocated knee would certainly require a pressure bandage, possibly a plaster cast.

"I'll see to all of that," the grim-faced senator informed his guests.

Three of them tried to speak at once, offering sage advice as ranking members of the DOJ, the FBI, and NYPD. Harlan Maddox raised a hand to silence them and took charge of the situation as he had at their first meeting, in the conference room at Foley Square, not quite two days ago.

"I'll deal with this," he told them, brooking no denials. "And I won't be pressing any charges."

"Senator," Adele Wainwright began, "a crime has been committed before law enforcement officers, another one confessed. It isn't up to you whether—"

"Quiet!" Maddox cut in, damming the rush of protests from his visitors. "Unless you all want trouble far beyond your wildest dreams, it is *entirely* up to me."

"But sir—" Duchene began to say.

"Enough!" Maddox half-shouted. "I'm the victim here, together with my daughter, and I mean to settle this my way. Obstruct me, and I promise you demotions at the very least, if it's the last thing that I ever do in office. Picture a committee looking into how the Bureau and AG's office has been blind to snuff films over *decades*. Call it negligence at best, and who knows what an oversight committee may discover after that? Complicity, perhaps? The very last thing either one of your department's need right now."

Chief Byrne seemed in a mood to stand his ground. "With all respect, Senator, NYPD doesn't dance to tunes from Washington."

"You're right, of course," Maddox replied. "The worst that I could do for you is have a private word with your Commissioner, a longtime friend of mine. Rather than jeopardize federal subsidies across the board to your department—tactical equipment from the U.S. military, funding for the local war on drugs, whatever—I suspect he might be willing to make changes in command, especially when it's revealed that ranking members have been sitting on their hands while foreign mobsters run around scot-free in the five boroughs."

Byrne's face colored, almost turning purple, but he closed his mouth without another word.

"All right, then," Maddox pressed on. "Here's what will happen if no one among you opts to scuttle his or her career. First, to the SFX team, I propose payment of the amount agreed upon at our last meeting. You've fulfilled our contract, saved my daughter's life, and for however long I may remain in office after this, you have my friendship, guaranteed."

Grant nodded thanks, saw no reason to answer verbally.

"As to the media," Maddox declared, "I will devise a story with some vague relationship to truth, sparing my daughter from intrusive inquiries while noting that my poor wife's mental state, already strained, has suffered a collapse, prognosis poor. There's a facility near Richmond that will take her in and offer counseling, but with the state she's in, it would be folly to release her until all concerned are confident that she's no danger to herself or others."

Grant managed to suppress a smile at that, one of the oldest tricks on record, going back to Old Joe Kennedy, one of his pesky children who had been lobotomized and spent her life confined for the most part, diagnosed as "mentally retarded," till her death at eighty-six, still hospitalized. Other renowned lobotomy recipients over the years included violinist Josef Hassid, actress-singer Alys Robi, artist Sigrid Hjertén and Hollywood matinee idol William Baxter, among many others.

"If we're all agreed, then?" Maddox asked the room at large. When no one spoke in opposition, he said, "Fine, then. I'll begin making arrangements right away, beginning with a house call from a doctor in the building to sedate Jolene. Agent, Duchene, if you're remove those cuffs?"

"Yes, sir?"

As they left The Majestic in Mahoney's rental car, to meet the other members of their team, Natalie said, "I don't like dropping it like this."

"Same here," Grant said. "At least we shut one network down, and who knows? If we happen on another one…"

"We'd need to deal with it," she said.

"My thoughts exactly," he replied.

If You Liked This, You Might Like:
Blood Sport: Special Agents Flynn and
Tanner, FBI (VICAP Book 1)

Los Angeles is city primeval, home base for the sociopathic elite. Charles Manson. The Hillside Strangler. And now—the Reaper. He hunts at night terrorizing whole families at gunpoint, mutilating and finally slaughtering them. Dozens of victims. No survivors. No Clues.

Special Agents Joe Flynn and Martin Tanner, are highly trained members of the Federal Bureau of Investigation's Violent Criminal Apprehension Program. But the Reaper never leaves a trace. Flynn and Tanner can do nothing except pace in the shadows of the sleeping city waiting for the Reaper to strike again.

The case files of Special Agents Flynn and Tanner are a scorching record of brutal crime. Their Los Angeles is an urban nightmare ruled by psychotic lords of violence. But VICAP agents are tough and resourceful—and they never give up.

Thought this series is fiction, VICAP is a real organization initially conceived in the late 1960s when the crimes of the Boston Strangler, Charles Manson, and other "motiveless" killers began to make national headlines.

AVAILABLE NOW

About the Author

A California native, Michael Newton has published 215 books under his own name and various pseudonyms since 1977. He began writing professionally as a "ghost" for author Don Pendleton on the best-selling Executioner series and continues his work on that series today. With 104 episodes published to date, Newton has nearly tripled the number of Mack Bolan novels completed by creator Pendleton himself.

Newton's first book under his own name was Monsters, Mysteries and Man (1979), a survey of unexplained phenomena for younger readers. While 156 of Newton's published books have been novels—including westerns, political thrillers and psychological suspense—he is best known for nonfiction, primarily true crime and reference books.